Murder Is Broadcast

Murder Is Broadcast

—A Rounders Mystery—

C L Hutchins

iUniverse, Inc.
Bloomington

Murder Is Broadcast
A Rounders Mystery

iUniverse books may be ordered through booksellers or by contacting:

iUniverse
1663 Liberty Drive
Bloomington, IN 47403
www.iuniverse.com
1-800-Authors (1-800-288-4677)

ISBN: 978-1-4759-7572-7 (sc)
ISBN: 978-1-4759-7574-1 (hc)
ISBN: 978-1-4759-7573-4 (e)

Library of Congress Control Number: 2013902494

Printed in the United States of America

iUniverse rev. date: 02/21/2013

Disclaimer

Some of the towns and places mentioned in this book exist, but all the characters and events are entirely fictitious and creations of the author's mind. The characters represent no one living or dead. Midway, the small cafe and gas station at the intersection of highways 30 and 218 in Eastern Iowa, was torn down several decades ago.

Dedication And Acknowledgements

This book is dedicated to members of my immediate family who are no longer living: My wife of 45 years, Carolyn Moran Hutchins, and my daughter Christie, who died in 2009 at the age of 37.

I wish to thank my two living daughters, Holly and Julie, for their support and understanding throughout the process of writing this mystery.

My appreciation extends to the many people in my life who helped me develop self-confidence and skills as I grew up in the 1950s. I especially remember the support and forbearance of Miriam Jeffrey and Paul Nielson, two of the many wonderful teachers I had during my time in high school.

Finally, I dedicate this book to everyone who enjoys reading mysteries.

List of Characters:

The Rounders

Fritz	Fritz McKay, sixty-two, widower, retired manager of a seed corn company, former mayor of Belle Plaine, close friend of Stoner
Lawrs	Lawrence Jensen, twenty-four, single, farmer, lady's man, jokester, lives near Newhall (nickname rhymes with 'stars')
Mac	Mackenzie Brownlee, sixty-three, owns Midway—a roadside cafe, gas station and motel on the Lincoln Highway, collects Native American artifacts, married to her second husband
Pansy	Frank O'Malley, fifty-one, married, runs an automotive garage in Belle Plaine, friend of Roy
Roy	Roy Mortensen, sixty-seven, divorced, amateur horticulturist, part-time lawyer, friend of Pansy, lives in Belle Plaine
Stoner	Mildred Stone, fourty-seven, widow, owns a lumberyard and hardware store in Blairstown, manages a farmer's grain co-op, close friend of Fritz

Others

Bill Robinson, farmer behind Truesdale
Clyde Martinek, small-time farmer, handyman
Shelia Martinek, Martinek's daughter
Everett Samuelson, lawyer in Vinton, good friend of Roy Mortensen
Jim Ross, lives across from Truesdale's farm, Lawrs' friend
John Truesdale, farmer near Blairstown, neighbor of Robinson and Ross
Ralph Kretzler, sheriff of Benton County
Ruthie Williamson, waitress at Midway
Sam Winfield, contract postman

Chapter One

Thursday, August 21, 1952

The Rounders met for coffee on Thursday mornings at Midway, a roadside cafe and gas station on the Lincoln Highway. Cedar Rapids was twenty miles east, and Belle Plaine was twenty miles west. The group's name came from the round table where they sat.

Built in 1922 as a speakeasy and brothel, the small bedrooms upstairs where young women plied their trade weren't used anymore. Mac—Mackenzie Brownlee, the owner of Midway—didn't like to think about what went on up there.

This particular Thursday morning, Ruthie Williamson, the cafe's only waitress, was standing behind the bar, listening to the morning *Arthur Godfrey Show* on an old radio. As she listened, an announcer broke in: "We interrupt this program to bring you a special news bulletin from WMT Radio."

Ruthie shouted across the cafe. "Hush up over there! There's a news announcement." She turned the volume up. The Rounders stopped talking and listened.

"We interrupt this broadcast to bring you late-breaking news. A man has been found murdered in his home on a farm south of Blairstown in Benton County. He was shot to death. Ralph Kretzler, the county sheriff, has identified the man as John Truesdale. No other details have been released. Stay tuned to WMT Radio for further news bulletins."

Lawrs—Lawrence Jensen, a young farmer in his mid-twenties, was the first to speak, "Jim Ross said Truesdale recently got in a fight with someone."

"Who's Jim Ross?" Roy Mortensen, a part-time lawyer and full-time amateur horticulturist, asked. He was sixty-seven.

"He owns the farm across from Truesdale's," Lawrs responded.

"Did he know the person?"

"No. They were behind the house. He couldn't hear what they were arguing about; it just sounded like they were about to come to blows."

"That doesn't surprise me. It was hard to get along with Truesdale," Fritz McKay said. He was a retired manager of a seed corn company and the former mayor of Belle Plaine. He was sixty-two, always the gentleman and well dressed. His only vice was that he was addicted to Mickey Spillane novels. "The police chief told me that he came into Kelley's Tavern a lot and usually got into arguments. One time it got so bad that Kelley had to throw him out."

"Who was he fighting with then?" Roy asked.

"It was a neighbor—Robinson was his name, I think."

Lawrs explained, "He owns the farm behind Truesdale."

"Could Robinson have killed him?" Mac asked. Most of the day, she sat at the round table where the Rounders met, watching the gas pumps through the front windows, talking to customers, and keeping her books. She collected and sold antiques displayed on shelves and tables around the cafe. She was sixty-three.

"What's Robinson like?" Roy asked.

Fritz replied, "I didn't know him, but the chief told me that he didn't start the fight with Truesdale. It was Truesdale who was hot under the collar."

"It's hard to believe it was Robinson," Lawrs said, "I've only met him a couple of times. He's a big, burly, rough-looking guy, but he seems nice—who knows?" He paused and joked: "Maybe he killed himself to escape the heat. It's been so damned hot over at my place you could fry eggs on my tractor."

It had been over one hundred degrees with high humidity for two weeks—not unusual for Iowa in August. People stopped at Midway because it had a window air conditioner. Most people had no air conditioning in their cars or homes. As Lawrs said once, you had to be a banker, a mortician, or a theater owner to have central air conditioning. After Mac bought her window unit, Lawrs facetiously asked her if he could get one with S&H Green Stamps. Stoner quickly told him that he couldn't. "If you could," she said, I'd have had one long ago."

Pansy smiled and nudged Lawrs, "Was Truesdale single? Did he get around like you do?" Pansy was a strange nickname for a man. No one knew how he got it; it didn't fit him. He was fifty-one, owned a garage in Belle Plaine, wore bib-overalls in the summer, and was a bit of an iconoclast. He liked to give Lawrs a hard time.

"All you old codgers think about is sex; get a life!" Lawrs said with a grin.

"Okay, but was he single?"

"I saw him with a girl from Blairstown a few months back. Her name's Shelia Martinek. I think they broke up since, but now she's pregnant. I don't know if Truesdale is the father."

"Is she related to Clyde Martinek?" Stoner asked. She had been uncharacteristically silent. Her name was Mildred Stone; she was forty-seven. Everybody just called her Stoner. It was as unusual a nickname for a woman as Pansy was for a man. But it suited her abrasive, forceful style. When her husband died, she continued to run their hardware store and lumberyard in Blairstown; she was also the manager of a local farmer's grain co-op.

"Yes," Pansy responded, "She's Old Man Martinek's daughter. Maybe he killed Truesdale because he got Shelia pregnant. I wouldn't put it past him; he has a terrible temper."

"He's a troublemaker, all right," Stoner said. "I've had run-ins with him at the co-op."

Roy asked, "What's he look like? I don't know him."

Stoner replied, "Nasty. Looks real mean. I lived in Chicago in the Twenties, and he looks like a gangster; you'd almost expect him to carry a submachine gun in his pickup's back window."

"Nice," Roy said.

Pansy spoke up, "Truesdale's uncle was in my garage a while back to have his pickup fixed. It was a 1948 dark blue F1 Ford; it had Ohio plates." Pansy always remembered every detail about a vehicle. "I didn't know who he was, but he told me that he was visiting his nephew, Truesdale."

Lawrs offered, "Jim, his neighbor, said Truesdale recently got his property appraised."

"That's because he was up to his ass in debt," Pansy said. "At least that's what the implement dealer told me. He holds a note on his farm for some equipment he sold him."

Mac objected, "Oh, come on, Pansy, let's be a little more genteel. Remember there are ladies present."

"Oh, yeah!" Pansy replied, "I forgot!" He laughed and lightly punched her arm.

"I can find out how much debt he has on his farm," Roy offered. "I can look it up next time I'm over at the courthouse."

"That'd be good," Pansy said. "Maybe how much he owed was related to his murder."

Ruthie came over with the coffee pot. She was twenty-one. Her blonde hair was short. She used red lipstick but no other makeup. She usually wore a skirt and sweater; at work she added a waist apron—unlike Mac, who wore a bib apron when she was behind the counter. Ruthie had crinoline slips for going out at night, but she seldom had a reason to wear them because she wasn't invited out often. She went first to Lawrs, "Lawrs, honey, want some more coffee?"

"He's your honey, uh?" Stoner asked.

"Oh, you know what I mean," Ruthie said dismissively. "Anybody else want some?"

"I guess we know where we are in the pecking order," Pansy said acerbically.

Stoner ignored the interaction and changed the subject. "Did anybody hear anything about the robbery at Dot's antique store over near Atkins?"

"The sheriff came in," Mac said. "He wanted to know if anyone had been in here trying to sell some of her stolen items."

"Did he describe the guy?" Fritz asked.

"No. Just said a neighbor saw a dark-colored pickup about the time of the robbery. Dot wasn't there at the time."

"Interesting," Pansy said. "Truesdale's uncle's pickup was dark blue. I wonder if there's a connection between the murder and the robbery?"

"The radio announcement didn't say if Truesdale had been robbed. I'll ask the sheriff," Fritz said. He had a good working relationship with Sheriff Kretzler from the time that he had been mayor of Belle Plaine.

"Goodness," Mac said. "You'd think we were a bunch of detectives. I can see the headlines now, 'amateur detectives solve farmer's murder.' We've already got four suspects: Truesdale's uncle, the robber at Dot's, Old Man Martinek, and maybe even Robinson. We'd better be careful, the sheriff will not take kindly to us butting in," Mac said.

"He's never going to solve it," Stoner asserted. "If someone stole his wife's cookie jar, he couldn't figure out who took it."

"That's not kind," Mac said.

Stoner continued her negative assessment of the sheriff, "Kretzler should have retired a decade ago. He's over seventy and needs to go to the old folks home. The county commissioners ought to appoint a new sheriff."

"It's not going to happen," Fritz said. "He's elected. As long as he keeps the voters happy, he'll stay in office. And take my word for it, he knows how to schmooze the voters."

"Well, I'll stick to my story," Stoner replied. "We have more brains in our collective pinky-fingers than he's got in his whole head."

In the middle of the discussion, Sam Winfield, the mailman, came in and put the mail on Mac's table. "Hi, everybody," he said. "Hear about the murder?" Everyone greeted him. Mac told him that they had heard the announcement on the radio.

As a rural postman, Winfield's route took him to Midway every morning. He worked under contract to the post office and drove a beat-up old pickup to deliver the mail. Pansy enjoyed poking fun at his pickup. Once, he said, "Well, I see you haven't washed it since the last snow."

Sam had jabbed back, "Oh, it's sort of like you, Pansy; I give it a bath once a year—whether it needs it or not."

Sam wasn't married although the rumor was that he had been once. He knew all his mail customers well, but as far as anyone knew, he never gossiped about them. He didn't have any close friends. He wasn't unfriendly; he just avoided social events. He lived on a small farm outside of Lucerne, but he leased his land out.

Mac asked Sam if he delivered mail to Truesdale.

"I do, but he doesn't get much."

"Did you meet his uncle when he was there?" Pansy asked.

"I knew he had a visitor. There was a pickup with Ohio plates behind his house for several days. Was that his uncle?"

"That's who it was," Pansy replied.

This particular morning, Sam stayed to listen to some of the conversation. It was a hard not to be interested in murder when it was so close to home. After awhile, however, he had to excuse himself in order to finish his mail route. He said the customers at the end of his route would be upset if he were late.

As Sam left, Roy got up and walked out with him. They looked strikingly different. Sam was tall and muscular, in his forties. Roy was short, somewhat fragile looking, and in his late sixties. It was hot today, so Sam was wearing a short-sleeved shirt and shorts. Roy wore wool pants year round and a long-sleeved dress shirt rolled up at the wrist. He didn't change his clothes often and looked frumpy.

Roy followed Sam out because four weeks earlier, he had agreed to do a small legal job for him. Since Roy didn't practice fulltime law anymore, he was always on the lookout for small cases that weren't too involved. Sam had offered him one. He wanted Roy to help identify his parents. A couple named Winfield had adopted him at birth, but they both had died recently. He wanted Roy to help him find his birth parents.

Roy had told him he would need to petition the district court to have his adoption records opened. When Sam asked him how much he would charge to do the work, Roy told him twenty-five dollars. Sam thought that was cheap and paid him upfront. Roy was always broke, so twenty-five dollars helped out.

Roy walked out with Sam today because he wanted to tell him that the court had not yet acted on their request to open the adoption records.

"Don't worry about it, Roy," Sam said. "I should have called you—I found out on my own. A cousin I didn't know I had tracked me down."

"How did he find you?"

"It was a she. She knew my mother had a child out of wedlock.

Somehow she knew the name of the couple that adopted me. Lucky for me, my cousin didn't give up until she found me."

"Great. Next time I'm at the courthouse, I'll withdraw the petition. Is that okay?"

"Absolutely," Sam said, "No reason to keep bothering anybody. Just keep the money I gave you." Sam got in his pickup and left. Roy was happy that he didn't want any of the money back.

When Roy returned to the table, they were talking about the break-in at Dot's again.

"If the burglar's smart," Mac said, "he's long gone. I'm just glad he didn't break in here and steal my artifacts." She pointed to several waist-high display cases that stood next to of the row of windows at the front of the cafe.

Mac never said much about the Native American artifacts she kept in the display cases. They weren't for sale. She treated them as museum pieces for the tourists. She collected them because she was one-quarter Meskawaki, a tribe sometimes called the Fox. Her grandparents had lived on the Fox and Sauk reservation near Tama, just west of Belle Plaine. She never told people about her heritage unless she knew them well.

"Who'd want that stuff anyway, Mac?" Pansy asked in his usual gruff manner.

"You'd be surprised. Things like that," she pointed to a beaded jacket in the closest glass display case, "can bring thirty dollars or more."

"You're kidding!" Lawrs was astonished.

"No, I'm not. In Santa Fe and New York where the big collectors are, they get more valuable every year. I don't want someone coming in here to hold me up. I'd appreciate if you didn't tell anybody."

"Our lips are sealed, Mac," Pansy said on behalf of everyone.

Roy changed the subject. "Civil Defense wants us all to build bomb shelters. They sent me a pamphlet. Any of you get one?"

"Who'd they send them too?" Pansy asked.

Stoner, who also served as the head of the county Red Cross, answered, "They asked me for the Red Cross mailing list. I wouldn't have sent it, but with all the talk about the Russian's nuking us, I decided it was okay. They also want us to promote a film that tells kids to 'duck and cover.'"

Roy asked, "What's that mean?"

"Just that if a bomb goes off, they should get under their desks and put their hands over their heads."

"Boy, that doesn't sound very safe," Mac asserted. "Just think what happened to Hiroshima."

"I agree," Fritz said. "And now we've got a hydrogen bomb. Did you see the pictures when they tested it in Nevada?" Several people nodded.

"I hate to think about what happens when the Russians get one," Pansy said. "It's just a matter of time, I'm sure."

"Any of you going to build a shelter?" Stoner asked.

"Nope. I figure if God is going to get me," Pansy volunteered, "He'll get me whether or not I'm in a shelter, and if He doesn't want me, I don't need a shelter anyway."

"I suppose you're right," Lawrs said, smiling. "But all the same, I'm glad my father put a storm cellar in our backyard. I can use it like a bomb shelter, and if I have a gal over when something like a tornado hits, we can go down there and be really safe."

"Yeah, safety comes first when you're dealing with gals you don't know—at least that's what they teach guys in the army," Pansy interjected with a Cheshire cat grin on his face.

"Oh, be still," Mac said. "Lawrs, you think about sex so much you must not get any on a regular basis."

"Oh! Got him!" Stoner said with glee.

"By the way," Pansy asked Lawrs, "when you have girls over in this hot weather, do you sleep under a blanket?"

"No, we sleep in the raw and use a fan," Lawrs responded.

"Doesn't that cause it to shrink up?" Pansy asked.

"Got him again!" Stoner said triumphantly.

Since it was time to go, Lawrs reminded everyone that he hadn't told his farmer joke for the day. It had become a ritual for him to tell one every time they met. Mac pretended she didn't like them, but she would repeat them to people who came into Midway for the next several days.

"This one's special; just for garage mechanics like you, Pansy," Lawrs said.

"Oh, thanks a lot," Pansy replied sarcastically.

Lawrs started, "This Iowa farmer named Homer met a rancher from Wyoming. Homer said he had a big, hundred-sixty acre farm. The rancher said, 'That ain't nothin'. My place is so big that when I start out in my pickup in the morning, I don't get to the other side of my ranch 'til the sun goes down.'" Lawrs paused. "Then Homer said, 'Yeah, I used to have a pickup like that, too.'" Everyone moaned.

Lawrs stayed for lunch. Unmarried, he didn't cook much at home.

Ruthie was always glad when Lawrs stayed for lunch. She had a crush on him, and she thought he was good-looking. He always wore jeans and t-shirts that emphasized his physique; he had a flattop. She flirted with him each time she waited on him. He never seemed to notice. From time to time, she would ask Mac how she could get him to pay more attention to her.

"Ruthie," Mac would say, "just stay away from him. He's playing the field and isn't ready to settle down. You don't want to become one of his girls. That wouldn't be good for your reputation. Once he's ready, he'll ask you out."

Ruthie wasn't so sure, and every Thursday when he came in, she'd try another approach. Today, she asked him if he liked going to drive-ins, hoping he might invite her to go to one.

"I don't like 'em," he said. "I prefer the regular theaters in Cedar Rapids or the King in Belle Plaine."

"Which theater do you like in Cedar Rapids? I like the Paramount. It's so glamorous; I just love all the gold, and the hall of mirrors makes it just like a palace or something."

"Oh, it's okay, but I also like the Iowa. Last time I was there I saw *The African Queen.*"

"I haven't seen it. Was it good?"

"Yeah, I like Humphrey Bogart. I especially liked *The Maltese Falcon.*"

"I haven't seen that either." He wasn't taking the hint. She'd have to come up with another plan for next week.

Chapter Two

Friday, August 22, 1952

Mac and Stoner decided to visit Dot's antique store near Atkins. They shared her interest in antiques, and they felt sorry for her because of the break-in. They also wanted to know about any possible connection between it and the murder of Truesdale.

Mac and Stoner had developed a slick scheme for buying antiques at a good price. They would drive Stoner's late model Cadillac up to a farmhouse about mid-morning when they the farmer would be out of the house. They would ask the farmer's wife if she had anything old to sell. —Everyone in Iowa had something old, and they always assumed it was valuable.

Because she saw them drive up in a Cadillac, the housewife hoped she could outfox the two rich women from town.

Stoner and Mac would make a fuss over everything the housewife showed them. They always bought something that had little value, but paid a little more than it was worth. That made the housewife feel good, and she would let her guard down.

That was important because, during their tour of the house, Mac and Stoner would spot something whose value the owner did not appreciate. As they were leaving, one of the them would say, "You know, that piece over there reminds me of one my mother had. I know it isn't worth much, but I'd love to have it for sentimental reasons." Then she would offer the housewife a small amount for the item, much less than it was worth.

Feeling smug about her earlier success, the housewife readily agreed to the price. That evening she would tell her husband how she had snookered two rich women from town.

Dot's antique store was a small, white, clapboard building on a gravel road; it was an old schoolhouse. She mostly carried collectables, the euphemism antique dealers used for stuff other people did not want.

Dot wasn't visible when they entered the store. They assumed she was in the storage area hidden from view by a curtain. After saying "Hello!" and "Yoo-hoo!" several times, Mac went through the curtain. The back door to the store was open, and Dot was standing outside by a large oil drum, burning rubbish.

"Dot. Hi there."

Dot turned around and saw Mac. She smiled broadly and said excitedly, "Oh, Mac! I'll pour some water on this fire and be right there." She was in her seventies and small, but she had carried a milk-pail full of water out with her. She tipped it into the barrel to extinguish the fire.

Coming through the door, she said, "It's so good to see you, Mac. How are you? I'd been going to come over to chat, but I've been so upset by the break-in. You know I was robbed, don't you?"

"Yes. I heard. I'm so sorry."

"The radio said yesterday a man was murdered over by Blairstown. I hope he wasn't the one who broke in here. I'm just glad I wasn't here when it happened." She paused and cautiously touched the side of an electric coffee pot. "Would you like some coffee? It's still hot."

"I'd love a cup. Stoner is with me; she'd probably like one, too."

"Stoner. How wonderful; I haven't seen her in ages." Dot always focused on the other person; she never asserted her own views. Mac was surprised she had the gumption to open a retail store.

By this time, Stoner had heard the two women talking; she came to the back of the store. "Dot, how are you? I heard about the break-in."

"Oh, it's so good to see you Stoner." Dot was smiling broadly. "I was just telling Mac I'm glad I wasn't here at the time. I could've been murdered like that man over by Blairstown."

"Did your neighbors see anything?"

"Myrtle said she thought she'd seen a pickup." She pointed in the direction of her neighbor's house.

"What color was it?"

"She said it was dark—blue or something." Mac remembered that Pansy had said Truesdale's uncle was driving a dark blue pickup.

"What all did they take?" Mac asked.

"Let's take our coffee to the table up front, and I'll tell you." She had put the coffee on a small tray. "Sorry the cups and saucers don't match—of course, they never do in a place like this." They laughed.

Once seated, Mac asked again, "Tell us what they stole."

"All my sterling silver. I had several serving pieces and two real nice flatware sets. They took a couple of pocket watches and some costume jewelry. All-in-all, it was probably worth two hundred dollars."

"That's a lot," Stoner sympathized. "Were you insured?"

"No. I've got a little policy on the building, but nothing on the antiques. It's my profit for several months. Things have been so slow I've considered closing down, but I figure I haven't anything better to do with my time."

Mac knew that Dot and her husband lived off a small social

security check and what he made doing odd jobs. But he was not well; he had had several small heart attacks. As a result, he couldn't work as much as he used to, so any income from the shop made a significant difference in their lives.

Stoner and Dot started talking about Depression glass; Stoner collected it. Dot took her to a shelf where she showed her a set of six, light-green, pressed-glass salad plates.

Mac started looking around other parts of the room. There was a little bit of everything: a box of discarded Simplicity and Butterick dress patterns, old phonograph records, *Reader's Digests*, discarded Christmas decorations, and so forth. It bothered Mac that people threw out so much. Raised in the Depression, she always had a 'waste not, want not' philosophy. She didn't think the younger generation as represented by Ruthie and Lawrs understood what the previous generation had gone through. For example, they had both given her a hard time about the old radio she had in the cafe. Lawrs was trying to convince her to buy a new radio that didn't have tubes; Mac told him that she would hang on to what she had until it didn't work. Ruthie had pushed for a jukebox with new, smaller records; 45s she had called them. Mac told her that she didn't want one. They looked too junky, like a lot of the new cars. In fact, she had wondered if the same guy that designed jukeboxes also designed cars for GM and Ford.

The only concession she'd made to modern entertainment had been to put a black and white television set at the end of the counter in the cafe. It had been a good for business in 1949 when she got it. People who didn't have sets would come in to watch TV shows like Milton Berle's and *What's My Line.* Mac didn't like Berle; she thought he was too corny and told too many New York jokes. She had heard there were now color sets. She accepted the fact that she would have to break down and buy one of them eventually—but not before the black and white one broke down.

On top of an old bureau, Mac spotted a small walnut box. It

had an old county history from Ohio in it. She remembered that Truesdale's uncle was from Ohio. She thumbed through the volume. She found an entry for a Truesdale family.

She had only started to skim the article when Dot and Stoner came over.

"What are you asking for this box?" Mac asked.

Dot replied, "I was asking four. But you can have it for two; that's what I paid for it. I got it at an auction back in Ohio when I was visiting my sister."

"This *History of Washington County* is interesting," she said, holding it up. "It's got a family called Truesdale in it."

"Isn't that the man that was murdered?" Dot asked.

"Yes," Mac answered. "But it's from the 1870s, so our Truesdale wouldn't be in it."

Dot added, "There's also an old family bible, an inventory of some kind, and some old pictures in it."

"I'll buy it," Mac said. "Even if there isn't a connection to Truesdale, it's a nice box; it will sell in my store. I'll pay you five; you've got it underpriced."

"Thanks, so much, Mac," Dot said appreciatively.

Stoner bought the Depression glass salad-set; she also paid Dot a little over her asking price. Like Mac, she felt sorry for her.

Dot patted both women on the arm and said, "Thanks so much; I appreciate it." They could tell she was trying hard not to cry.

Mac said, "Well, we've got to be getting along. I need to get back to give Ruthie her morning break. It's good to see you looking so well, Dot. So sorry about your loss."

Dot thanked them profusely, and they said goodbye.

They took their purchases to Mac's car. It was a 1948 Chrysler Windsor sedan. It was two-toned, with a lime-green bottom and a pastel blue-green—almost turquoise—top. Mac didn't drive it much. She didn't often leave Midway.

As soon as they were in the car, Mac told Stoner, "That county history in the box I bought might connect the Truesdale family in Ohio with the Iowa Truesdales. Lot's of old Iowa families came from Ohio, especially from around Marietta—which is in Washington County. I didn't have time to look, but the old bible may have some clues, too—there's a genealogy in the back."

Do you think there's any connection between Dot's break-in and Truesdale's murder?" Stoner asked.

"If the pickup was dark blue, maybe. We should ask Pansy to go see Dot's neighbor; maybe he could prompt her memory—especially to see if it had an Ohio plate."

"Good idea," Stoner said. "Why don't you call him? I'll tell Fritz; he might want to tell the sheriff."

"Speaking of Fritz," Mac asked, "are you and he still seeing a lot of each other?"

"We get together every week or so. Sometimes he comes to my house for supper; sometimes I go to his. We like to go to dances at Ced-Rel."

"That's that club on the west side of Cedar Rapids, isn't it? Mac asked."

"Yes."

"Do you go to the movies very often?"

"Yeah, once a month or so. We like the first runs at the Paramount. We saw *An American in Paris* a few months ago; it was wonderful. Last weekend, we went to the Iowa Theater and saw *A Street Car Named Desire.* It was awful. That Brando was just an animal, and he was so brutal to Vivien Leigh. I have no idea what this world is coming to."

Do you think you and Fritz might ever get married?"

"I doubt it. We're just good friends. Although, it would be nice to have somebody around when I get older. Neither one of us has kids, so there aren't going to be too many people who'll care what happens to us on down the line."

"Stoner! How can you say that? You've got a lot of friends. What would Blairstown do without you?"

"It's not the same thing, but I suppose."

Mac dropped Stoner off at her home and went back to Midway. She called Pansy and asked him if he could go over to Dot's neighbor and try to get a better description of the truck the robber used. Pansy said he would go see her when he got a chance.

Chapter Three

Saturday, August 23, 1952

Several hours after the lunch trade had died down, Mac sat alone at her round table. She was depressed.

Truesdale's death brought back memories of how her son, Todd, had died.

He had gotten into a fight and had been shot in a bar in Rock Springs, Wyoming when he was twenty-four. The murder brought it all back.

She and Todd's father, Jacob Steele, her first husband, had married in Tama when she was sixteen. He had trouble finding work there, and a friend had helped him find a union job in a coalmine in Rock Springs. It was dirty and dangerous work.

In 1913, he quit and got a job as a fireman for a railroad that ran passenger and freight service between Casper, Wyoming and Denver, Colorado.

They moved to Casper, and Todd was born a year later.

In 1923, when Todd was nine, the passenger train that Jacob was working on crossed a trestle that had been undermined by strong rains. The trestle collapsed, and the train plunged to the bottom of the ravine. He and twenty-nine others were killed.

To support herself, Mac worked as a waitress in Casper. It was a hard life, nothing like the lives of the families portrayed on the popular television shows that Ruthie like to watch such as *Ozzie and Harriet* or *Leave It To Beaver*. In real life, she would tell Ruthie, mothers worked outside the home, not everybody got a long with each other, and fathers weren't always the heroes of the family. Ruthie never contradicted Mac, but she was determined she would be like June Cleaver and her husband would be like Ward. Her sons would be David and Ricky Nelsons; her daughter would be a Kathy Anderson.

In 1933, Mac moved back to Iowa and bought Midway, using the money she had saved from the settlement the railroad had given her when Jacob died.

Todd was nineteen at the time, but he didn't like Iowa, especially the isolation of Midway. He moved back to Wyoming a year later. It was still the Depression, and work was hard to find. Fortunately, he was able to get a job in the same mine in Rock Springs where his father had worked. That is where he was living at the time that he was shot.

In 1942, when she was fifty-four, Mac married Thomas Brownlee, a long-haul trucker. He frequently stopped at Midway and had gotten to know her. He was single and had no children. Mac liked him and accepted his proposal of marriage.

She wasn't bothered by the fact he was gone for days at a time. In fact, she was glad he wasn't always there; she had gotten used to making it on her own since Jacob died.

She thought of herself now as an old lady. She frequently didn't put on any makeup. She was five-foot seven and wore size 14 printed rayon dresses. She wore lace-up shoes with thick heels; she referred to them as her nurse's shoes in black—others called them 'granny' shoes.

As she sat at her big round table, she knew she would go to her grave thinking about the loss of her only child.

She wondered if Truesdale's mother was still alive. She knew how hard his death would be on her. Would there be a funeral for him in Iowa? Or would they send his body back to wherever he had previously lived? Was he from Ohio as his uncle was? She wondered again if there could be a connection between the box she had bought at Dot's and the murder of Truesdale.

She decided to call Charles Patterson, the Vinton funeral director that had taken care of Todd's funeral.

When he answered, she said, "Charles, this is Mac over at Midway. I assume you know about John Truesdale?" She didn't wait for an answer. "He came in here sometimes." That was not true, but it gave her a credible excuse for asking about the funeral arrangements. "I thought I'd pay my respects. Will there be a viewing at your place? Will they bury him around here?"

She listened as Patterson told her that Truesdale was from Ohio; the family wanted his body shipped there. "Besides," he added, "he was killed by a shotgun blast at close range; there won't be an open-casket."

"Are his parents alive?" she asked. Patterson told her that they were both dead. His mother had died just a few months earlier; he had handled arrangements for her burial. She had been living with Truesdale on his farm at the time.

"Is there a large family?"

"Just two cousins and an uncle in Ohio. I gather the uncle had been back here, visiting Truesdale. But his kids say he hasn't come home. They don't know how to reach him to tell him his nephew's dead."

She thanked Patterson and hung up.

It seemed strange that Truesdale's uncle had not gone home after he left Truesdale's farm. What had happened to him? She had an uneasy feeling about it. Did he kill Truesdale and run away?

She sat for another hour at her table, not focusing on anything.

Chapter Four

Monday, August 25, 1952

Mac wasn't the only one who had a hard time processing the information about Truesdale's murder and dealing with the memories it brought back. Roy Mortensen had a daughter living in Florida with her mother, Roy's ex-wife. He hadn't seen or heard from his daughter or her mother since they left Chicago one year after they were married. That was in 1923. As a result, it was as if his daughter were dead, just as Mac's son was.

Roy was born to a well-to-do couple in Belle Plaine. His father had a successful law practice and built a building on Main Street. The family name, 'Mortensen,' was even cut into a stone marquee at the top of the building.

Roy had wanted to be a doctor. However, his father had insisted that if Roy expected him to pay for college, he would have to go to law school—specifically, Harvard, where he had gone.

Reluctantly, Roy did go to Harvard. After he graduated, his father bought him a law practice in Chicago. That is where he had met his wife. When the marriage fell apart, Roy closed the Chicago office, moved to Belle Plaine, and tried, without much success, to practice law there.

When his father died, the estate was large—by small town standards. Roy wanted to invent something: he decided he would build a plant that turned corncobs into plastic. Scientists had shown that it could be done; he had read about it in the *Wall Street Journal.*

He built a small plant by the railroad tracks in Belle Plaine. However, he couldn't get the technical people he needed to run the plant to live in Belle Plaine—they could make more money in the cities. As a result, the endeavor failed. He lost his money. The building stood, abandoned, along the railroad tracks, near the roundhouse and switching yard.

Looking for something to do, he threw his energy into raising flowers; it was a passion he had shared with his mother. He created new hybrids— roses, peonies, and iris. His role model was Luther Burbank, a well-known horticulturist from the early part of the century; he had created hybrids such as the Shasta daisy.

To make money, he would create a new rose and give it the name of a rich woman, usually one that lived on the East Coast or near Chicago. He would write the woman and tell her that he had just named a new rose after her. He would offer to send her a free plant. She always accepted. Roy was counting on her to brag to her rich friends that a rose had been named for her and talk them into buying additional roses from him. His scheme usually worked.

He lived in an old house near downtown Belle Plaine. It was small and run down, but he seemed not to notice. He was a terrible housekeeper. There was only one path through the house: from the backdoor, through the kitchen and the dining room, and on to the front room that served as an office. The path was defined by stacks of old newspapers, law books, and books on horticulture. He never threw anything out.

Roy wore the same clothes day in and day out. He wore a Panama straw hat, summer and winter. It had been an expensive hat in its day, but now it was somewhat dirty and no longer held its shape.

He had no car. Getting around Belle Plaine without one was not a problem; everything was within walking distance. The only time that he needed a car was when he went to Vinton, the county seat, to do something related to his limited law practice. He usually didn't get there more than once a month—if that. He'd either hitch a ride with someone, or he'd take the bus.

Despite his shortcomings, Roy was liked and respected by all who knew him. He especially enjoyed the Rounders. Their Thursday morning meetings were the one social activity he had—other than visiting Pansy at his garage.

Pansy and Roy had developed a strong friendship. Although Pansy only had a high school education, he was an avid reader. He subscribed daily to the *Wall Street Journal* and the *Chicago Tribune.* Roy would borrow the newspapers, and the next time that he saw Pansy, they would have a lengthy discussion about some world or national problem both had read about. Pansy was the source of the newspapers piled throughout Roy's house.

Roy and Pansy also had discussions based on Roy's extensive reading in the local Belle Plaine Public Library. Recently he'd found Riesman's *The Lonely Crowd* and Mill's *White Collar.* He and Pansy agreed with their premise that society was moving more and more toward comformity, reducing individual initiative and control.

He also read histories. He particularly enjoyed presidential histories. Over the years, he had collected presidential signatures, starting with William Howard Taft. He would write each new President with a comment or question on some important issue of the day. If he didn't get a signed response, he'd keep writing until he did.

For his contribution to the Rounders' inquiries into Truesdale's murder, Roy decided he would take the bus to Vinton, and he would do a title search on Truesdale's farm. He wanted to see who had owned it in the past, and what liens there were against the title. He also thought it might be useful to look at the probate records for Truesdale's mother and father—if there were any.

The bus left at nine-fifteen; there were two stops. It got to Vinton about ten-thirty.

First he went to the county recorder's office in the courthouse to find the name of the current owner of Truesdale's farm. In all probability, it was Truesdale. But he wanted to check.

The courthouse was designed in a modified Neoclassical Revival style, without pillars or porticos. It was two stories tall with a large clock tower topped by a rounded dome; above that was a smaller cone with a flagpole above. The ceilings were high, about twenty steps from the first to the second floor. Fortunately for Roy, the recorder's office was on the first floor, only about fifteen steps up from the front entrance.

Entering the recorder's office, Roy faced a long counter; behind it, two clerks sat. Beyond them, was the large, walk-in vault where the property records were kept. Marriage and birth records were also kept there.

A middle-aged woman got up from her desk and came to the counter when Roy entered.

"Well, long time no see, Roy!"

"Hi, Jessie, how've you been? You're looking good, as usual."

"Flattery will get you everywhere, Roy. What do you need?"

"I want to look at the property records."

"Sure, come on back. Everything is in the vault. The plat maps are on the table to the right. When you're done, just put the volumes you pulled on the same table. I'll re-file them."

"Don't trust me to put them back?"

"I wouldn't have a job if I didn't have something to do," she said with a smile. "Besides, sometimes they get put in the wrong place, and it takes forever to find them."

Roy walked behind the counter to the large vault. It looked as though it came from a Hollywood movie. The rectangular, black steel door had to be nearly eight inches thick. It had two massive hinges. The vault was opened using a combination lock that released a large wheel that withdrew the bolts from the top and sides of the door.

After thanking Jessie, he walked into the vault. First, he looked in the large book that held the county plat maps. Every township was shown on a separate map. Each map showed all the properties in the township. Each property was numbered and, in addition, the current owner's name was written directly on it in pencil. When a property changed hands, the owner's name was erased; the new owner's name was written in its place. To get a list of the previous owners, Roy looked up the property number in a set of large books at the back of the vault.

As he suspected, John Truesdale's name was show as the current owner. A Vinton bank held the first mortgage. An individual held a second. An implement dealer from Belle Plaine held an additional lien. Roy guessed that the total of these three debts meant that Truesdale had almost no equity in the farm—if any.

Roy looked to find the names of the previous owners. Just before Truesdale, a Sarah and Ralph Truesdale had owned the property. He assumed they were Truesdale's parents.

The owner before that was Sarah Caldwell. He guessed that was Truesdale's mother's maiden name. She had probably inherited the property from her parents, Joseph and Marie Caldwell, the owners before her. Sarah must have deeded joint title to her husband, Ralph, when she married him.

When he was done, Roy put the books on the table just inside the door to the vault. He thanked Jessie as he left.

He went upstairs. The clerk of the court's office was just like the recorder's office below it. Even the vault looked the same. He talked with the woman who sat at the desk behind the counter; he told her what he needed. She took him to the vault and showed him where to look things up.

He started with the index of the abstracts of the probated wills. He found the numbers attached to each of the wills and the estate records for Truesdale's mother, father, and grandparents.

He found nothing unusual about the abstract of Ralph's will. The same was true for his wife, John's mother, Sarah. Sarah's will indicated that all her property and assets were to be 'divided equally among her living children.' Roy knew she had only had one child and was too old to have more children when the will was written, so he assumed that particular phrase was there because some lawyer wanted to cover all the bases. He then found the estate records for Joseph and Marie Caldwell. The records confirmed that they were the parents of Sarah, mother of John Truesdale.

Finished, he walked across the courthouse square to the office of his friend, Everett Samuelson. They had attended law school at Harvard at the same time; they had even been roommates for one year.

Samuelson' law office was dramatically different from the living room Roy used for his office. There was a waiting room for clients and a secretary. Down a hall were two offices, a law library, and a workroom.

Everything about Everett was professional. He was handsome in an older, statesman-like way; he was always immaculately dressed. Roy knew he was devoted to his wife and children. He always appeared interested in what others said, listening to them carefully. He genuinely liked the people he met, a trait Roy wished that he possessed. He was a defense attorney, a good one.

It was hard for Roy to deal with the fact that his life had turned out so differently than Everett's. He was just appreciative that Everett never seemed to judge him for the choices that he had made.

Everett and Roy talked about the usual things, including what every discussion in Iowa had to include, the weather. Everyone with any connection to farming, no matter how remote, began most conversations with reference to the weather. It was always too hot, too cold, too dry, or too wet; it was never just right.

They also discussed politics. Samuelson was as strong a Republican as Roy was a Democrat, so their discussions usually turned into friendly arguments. Today, they talked about the presidential election between Adlai Stevenson and Dwight Eisenhower.

"Stephenson should have run for governor again, not president," Everett said.

"I don't know about that," Roy responded. "But, I feel sorry for Kefauver. He should have had the nomination. He swamped Truman in New Hampshire, and he beat Stephenson in the other primaries."

Everett replied, "Stevenson's just too liberal for most folks; he's a bit of an egg-head."

"He may be a little academic, but don't pick on the fact he doesn't have much hair;" Roy smiled as he ran his hand over his thinning hair. "Maybe he should have been the one to wear a coonskin cap instead of Kefauver." Both men laughed.

"Whether it's Stevenson or Eisenhower, I for one, will be sorry to see Truman go," Roy said. "He was always so down to earth and direct. Remember when he fired back at that music critic because he complained about Margaret's singing?"

"Yes, didn't he say something like he'd need a beef stake for his eye and a supporter for below when he got through with him?"

"Something like that. And I always admired him for the way he stood up to MacArthur; he was such an arrogant man. If he'd had his way, we'd have had an all-out war with China."

"Yes, I agree, but now Truman will just fade away like MacArthur."

Finally, they got around to the murder. Samuelson knew quite a bit about the sheriff's investigation, but he didn't know that Truesdale's uncle had been visiting Truesdale before he died. He also didn't know that he had visited Pansy to have his truck fixed. He suggested they go over to the sheriff's office after they were done having lunch to be sure that he knew about the visit and the truck.

Roy was no fan of the sheriff and the feelings were mutual, but he agreed to go; it would be easier if Samuelson came along.

After lunch—a long one, Samuelson paid for both meals as he always did. Roy thanked him, jokingly saying that Samuelson was the successful one of the pair, and he was by most standards.

They walked to the sheriff's office in the courthouse. It was on the ground floor.

After greeting the sheriff, Samuelson said, "You know Roy Mortensen, I'm sure."

"Oh, Roy." Kretzler said, almost as if he hadn't seen him. "Good to see you. We've had a little excitement down in your part of the county." Obviously, he was referring to Truesdale's murder.

Roy said, "That's why I'm here. I told Everett I'd found out that Truesdale's uncle visited him just before he died; he was driving a dark blue Ford pickup like the one used to rob Dot over in Atkins."

"How do you know that?"

"Frank O'Malley over in Belle Plaine—you know, Pansy; he runs a garage over there. Frank said that a few days before the murder, the uncle brought the pickup in to be fixed."

"We know Truesdale had an uncle," the sheriff said summarily. "A neighbor told us the uncle had been visiting him just before he was murdered, and, of course, we know he had a vehicle." From the way he said vehicle, rather than pickup, Roy guessed the sheriff hadn't known what it was. "And," the sheriff added officiously, "It isn't connected to the break-in at Dot's."

Samuelson asked, "I understand the uncle is missing. Have you found him or his pickup?"

"No," the sheriff said. "We know where he comes from in Ohio, and we've contacted the chief of police over there. They're tracking him down and getting us a description of the vehicle." That confirmed for Roy that the sheriff didn't know what kind of vehicle Truesdale's uncle drove.

"Do you think the uncle could have killed Truesdale?" Samuelson asked.

"That's not a matter we can discuss at this time," the sheriff pronounced pompously.

"Is he the person who had the argument with Truesdale just before he died?" Roy asked.

"How'd you know about that?" the sheriff asked with some anger in his voice.

"Through a friend," Roy replied.

"What friend?" The sheriff demanded.

"Oh, you wouldn't know him," Roy answered. It was clear that the interview was at an end.

The men shook hands, and Roy and Samuelson left. As they walked across the courthouse square, Samuelson asked, "If the uncle is involved, I wonder what his motive was?"

"It wasn't property," Roy said. "From what I found in the clerk's office, he had no equity in that property. The uncle wouldn't have anything to gain by killing him. It would have to be a different motive."

They bid goodbye to each other, and Roy walked to the bus station. After he was on the bus, he realized that he had forgotten to tell the district judge's law clerk that he was withdrawing the request to open Sam Winfield's adoption records. He'd have to do it on another trip back to Vinton.

Chapter Five

Tuesday, August 26, 1952

Stoner had taken over the lumberyard and hardware store when her husband died suddenly of heart failure; apparently, it had been caused by an attack from a swarm of bees in his backyard.

They had no children, but she did have two small Pekingese dogs she doted on; she called them 'Sweet' and 'Sour' because of their contrasting dispositions.

She had been raised on the south side of Chicago. When she was young, her parents had sent her to live with her grandmother in Iowa; they had wanted to reduce her chances of being exposed to the 1918 flu epidemic that eventually killed more than a half a million people in the United States. Shortly after she had gone to Iowa, both of her parents had caught the flu and had died.

When she returned to Chicago, she had lived with an aunt. To support herself, she had taken a job as a 'taxi dance girl' in a Chicago dance hall. The name came from the fact that a man could dance with one of the girls for two minutes at ten cents a dance. They were not prostitutes, not at least in Stoner's case. Her boss would have fired any girl he thought had been selling her favors.

Stoner had met her husband at the dance hall. He had been

working on the construction of Chicago's Union Station. He had been from North Central Iowa, near the town where Stoner had stayed with her grandmother. As a young man from the country, working in a strange, big city, the dance hall had been one of the few places he could meet a girl.

When his work had come to an end, they had borrowed money from Stoner's aunt and bought the hardware store in Blairstown.

After she was widowed, she never thought of dating. However, she and Fritz McKay had gradually become close friends, starting from their initial contact at a Rounders' meeting. Fritz was tall and distinguished looking. She was much shorter and heavier, so people sometimes called them 'Mutt and Jeff'—out of their earshot, of course. Fritz was considerably older than Stoner, but that didn't bother either of them.

WHEN STONER GOT BACK FROM Dot's, she thought about what Lawrs had said about Shelia Martinek—that she was pregnant, and that John Truesdale may have been the father of her child. If that were true, it would give her father a motive to kill Truesdale.

Stoner knew that Martinek had a quick temper and was capable of blowing up at anyone. She had seen it firsthand. When he brought corn to the grain elevator every fall, he frequently shouted at her. The argument always focused on the weight of his truck. The empty weight had to be known because the weight of the grain it carried could only be determined accurately by subtracting the weight of the grain-loaded truck from its empty weight. For no reason that made sense, Martinek never would allow the empty truck to be weighted. As a result, Stoner used an estimate of the truck's weight based on information provided by the manufacturer for the year and model of the truck.

He would shout that the weight she used was too heavy. He

became so angry sometimes that he scared her. She had considered going to the co-op's board to get its members to let her refuse to accept Martinek's grain in the future.

His temper was so explosive, she believed he was capable of murdering Truesdale if he thought Truesdale had gotten his daughter pregnant. Stoner decided that the best way way to get to the heart of the matter of Shelia's pregnancy would be to talk with the girl in person. She worked at the Happy Farmer, a small cafe in Belle Plaine, so Stoner made a trip to the cafe.

When she got there, the cafe was hot. Fans were blowing everywhere, but the heat of the cooking made it even hotter than it was outside. In the winter, that was great, but in August, it limited the number of people willing to come in.

When Stoner arrived, there were only two men in the cafe, sitting on the red, vinyl-covered stools at the linoleum-covered counter. There were empty stools beside them, but Stoner chose a booth because she was, as she sometimes described herself, 'pleasingly plump.'

"Hi, Shelia," Stoner said as the girl came over with a menu. She looked hard: she had on too much makeup, she wasn't wearing stockings, and she hadn't shaved her arms or legs. Clearly, she was several months pregnant. Stoner thought she could be attractive with a little less makeup; without the stringy, dirty-blonde hair; and with better personal grooming. Her uniform could also benefit from being washed and pressed.

"What do you want?" Shelia said as she dropped a menu on the table.

"What's your special?"

"Meatloaf, gravy, mashed potatoes, and green beans," Shelia said, abruptly. "A dollar and a quarter; includes your drink. We got pie, too. What do you want to drink?"

"Iced tea, I think," Stoner said as she surveyed the menu. "The meatloaf sounds good, but I've got some in my ice box right now. I'll take the pork tenderloin sandwich with slaw."

"You bet," Shelia said. She was chewing Clove gum and made it pop; Stoner could smell it.

About ten minutes later, Shelia came back, carrying a sandwich with the breaded pork extending far beyond the margins of the bun; Stoner loved the crunchiness of the deep-fried crust on the meat.

Before Shelia could leave, Stoner asked, "Shelia, I see you are going to have a blessed event. When are you due?"

"Three months. Suppose you heard who the dad is," she said in a matter-of-fact way.

"Not really," Stoner replied.

"Truesdale, the guy that just got hisself killed. We were seeing each other; planning to get married next month."

Stoner didn't believe for a minute that Truesdale would marry her, given his temper and their age difference. To be kind, she said, "Oh, I had no idea. That's so sad. I feel bad for you. I know your dad will help you out."

"He's been a son-of-a-bitch; that's what he's been," she blurted out loudly. The two men at the counter swung around on their stools to stare at her. "Before John was shot, dad said he'd kill him. He went over there to have it out. Imagine, the guy who's going to be your son-in-law and you're gonna murder him!"

"Oh, that's awful. Surely, he didn't mean it," Stoner said.

"Yeah, he did. He went over and they had it out," she said decisively.

"I'm sure he was just saying that because he was upset," Stoner said.

"Maybe. After he was dead, dad said it was too bad he didn't get him first."

"Are you still living with your dad?"

"Mom," she said in her abbreviated style. "Dad threw me out.

Said he wasn't going to help me. Can you imagine? Said I was a whore—his own daughter, a whore. Imagine!" The two men at the counter were still listening intently.

She continued, "I'll have to work 'til the baby comes and go back right away. Mom's gonna watch it."

"Shelia, I'm so sorry to hear that. I'll keep you in my prayers, dear." Stoner was not a religious woman, as anyone who knew her would know, but it was about all she could think to say under the circumstances.

As she drove home, she decided to tell Fritz what she had heard.

When he answered the phone, she explained what Shelia had told her. She asked him what she should do. He told her to call the sheriff. She responded, "But you know him better than I do."

"No," he replied firmly. "You should call him. Information like that is more credible if it comes from the person involved."

After she hung up, she reluctantly called the sheriff. She didn't like the man, and she didn't trust he would do anything. After he had answered and she had identified herself, she said, "Sheriff, I'm not trying to stick my nose in where it is not wanted, but I thought you should know: I talked with Shelia Martinek today over where she works in Belle Plaine. She's clearly pregnant, and she told me the father was John Truesdale. She said it loud enough everybody in the cafe could hear. To make matters worse, she said her dad had threatened to kill him, and that they'd had an argument just before he died. Her words were 'they had it out.' I asked if she thought he meant it, and she told me that he did—although, later he told her something like 'I just didn't get to him in time.' Did you know about this, sheriff?"

The sheriff told her that he didn't know that Shelia was pregnant or that she was telling people the father was Truesdale. He also hadn't heard that Martinek had threatened Truesdale. He said he would follow up. The sheriff thanked Stoner for calling and hung up. She felt a bit better about him after he promised he would follow up—although she wondered how quickly and thoroughly he would do so.

She decided to save her big discovery until the Rounders' meeting.

Chapter Six

Wednesday, August 27, 1952

Lawrs decided to visit Jim Ross to get additional information about the argument Truesdale had with another man just before the murder.

Lawrs and Jim knew each other because they frequently drove to Iowa State football games together. They had both attended the ag school there, although at different times; Ross was a few years older than Lawrs.

Ross had red hair. He was stocky and a bit shorter than Lawrs. He was married and had two young children. He shared Lawrs interest in farming jokes.

Lawrs was driving his 1951 Chevrolet hardtop; it was blue with a white top. Most of the time, he drove a pickup, but he enjoyed using the Chevy in other situations, such as going to dances and football games. He knew Jim wouldn't think he was putting on airs by driving it to his place.

When he pulled into the yard, the barn doors were open; he could see Jim working on his tractor, an almost-new Allis-Chalmers. When he saw Lawrs, Jim put down his tools and came to the front of the barn, cleaning his hands on a rag as he walked.

"Jim," Lawrs said, "think we'll get any relief from this heat?"

"Let's hope it breaks soon," he said as he reached out to shake Lawrs' hand. "September should be better."

"I imagine that your family's still upset by Truesdale."

"Yeah. It's been hard for the women. My daughter is scared that someone's going to break into her room. Her brother's more interested in the blood and guns. The little devil—he keeps running around at night, acting like he's a ghost, scaring his sister to death. We just hope they catch the guy that did it soon."

"You said you'd heard someone having an argument with Truesdale; right?"

"Yeah, a couple of days before they found him. I never saw the guy. They were behind the house, back where John parked his car; I didn't even see what the guy came in. The argument went on maybe five minutes. It was pretty loud. I was in the front, cutting weeds. I was too far away to hear specifically what they were saying."

"Was his uncle there at the time?"

"I don't know. He parked behind the house, too, so I couldn't tell when he left."

"Who's taking care of the place?"

"Bob Rath. Do you know him?"

"Sure."

"Bob came in every couple days to help Truesdale when he was alive; he's been here every day since he died. Someone's going to have to do something pretty soon, though. Bob said he hasn't been paid. I'd be willing to help out, but I don't want to take total responsibility."

"I understand. Maybe other folks would pitch in. We could take turns until somebody decides what to do." Lawrs added, "The Ferguson boys would probably be willing to help."

Jim said, "There's enough feed for the cattle for a while, but the corn's gotta come in pretty soon. I don't want the responsibility for that, though I'm willing to help."

"We should ask a lawyer about any liability we'd incur. I see Roy Mortensen every week," Lawrs suggested. "He's a lawyer, I can ask him."

Jim couldn't resist; with a perfectly straight face he said, "You see a lawyer every week? Boy, you must be in more trouble than I guessed. How many girls have you got pregnant now?"

"Oh, come on. You know I meet a bunch of folks over at Midway every week just to talk. Roy's just one of the crowd. And for your information, none of my lady friends has ever gotten pregnant."

"Yeah, well, that's good to hear. I just have to keep you on your toes."

Lawrs smiled and changed the subject, "If you think it's okay, I'm going over and look around. I'm about at a point I could use more land. I'd let someone live in the house, feed his own cattle, and share the crops with me. Maybe Bob would be interested."

"Bob's a hard worker. I'm sure he doesn't have enough to buy a place, but it would be a great way for him to get started. The estate would have to get cleared up first, wouldn't it?"

"Yeah, I'm probably jumping the gun. Maybe the heirs would rent it out. Let me know if they show up, will you?"

"You bet."

"Jim, I'll let you get back to work. Can I leave my car here? Is the house is unlocked?"

"I'm pretty sure it's not locked, and there's no problem leaving your car here. If my wife comes out, I'll tell her that I bought her a new car." Lawrs laughed.

"Oh, that reminds me," Lawrs asked, "do you know how you can tell if you're a farmer?"

"Probably not," Ross said, knowing he had been set up for a joke.

"It's when your dog rides in your truck more than your wife does."

"I can top that," Ross replied. "Did you hear the one about the farmer and the bug that flew into his barn?"

"Nope."

"Well, the farmer was milkin' his cow. He'd just got a good rhythm going when a bug started circling his head. Suddenly, it flew into the cow's ear. The farmer didn't think much about it 'til the bug squirted out into his bucket. It went in one ear and out the udder."

"That's a dog of a joke," Laws laughed.

"Speaking of dogs, John's dog is chained out back by the chicken coop. He used to run free, but a couple of days before he died, John tied him out there. He'll bark, but he's not dangerous, especially if you feed him. There's dog food in a waste can by the back door. Give him some, and you'll have a friend for life. By the way, Truesdale called him Dog, just Dog. That was typical of him."

"Thanks for the tip," Lawrs shouted back as he walked across the road. The dog was already barking. He decided to ignore it for a few minutes.

First, he walked the perimeter of the yard, looking out over the cropland. It wasn't as good as the land on his place. From his days at Iowa State, he knew that the fertility of the land depended on where the ice-age glaciers melted, dumping their rich load of topsoil. The areas the glaciers didn't reach were rougher, and the soil wasn't as good. That explained why the land north of the Lincoln Highway was better than some of the land further south, where the glaciers reached some places, but not others. A ravine that ran behind the property testified to its roughness.

Truesdale's cattle were grazing in the field beyond the barn. Lawrs could see the pig lot as well, and beyond were farrowing sheds for the gestating and nursing sows.

He walked into the barn. It was three-stories. The lowest level ran down toward the ravine; it was open on two sides so that the cattle could come and go at will, depending on the weather. The second level opened onto higher ground at the same level as the house. Cows would have been milked there—if Truesdale had had any. Higher yet was the hayloft.

Lawrs could tell the barn wasn't in good shape. There were shingles missing from the roof. Some of the siding was loose; it was even missing in a couple of places.

His next stop was the corncrib. It was two-sided, corn on one side and oats on the other. You could park a tractor and a wagon in the middle. Sliding doors at each end allowed the tractor and wagon to enter and exit without backing-up. Truesdale's old John Deere tractor was there. The level of the corn was low. The oat bin was about three-quarters full.

Lawrs decided he would look inside the house. It was called an American Foursquare: two stories with four equal sides. The roof rose to a central peak with a chimney on top. A covered porch ran across the entire front of the house. It was reached by walking up six steps, indicating that the main floor was at that height.

He didn't even try the front door; he assumed it was locked. Most people never used their front doors. Instead, they entered through a side or back door. In this case, there was a side door at ground level. A small stoop hovered over the door.

Once inside, you could walk up six steps to the main floor or an equal number of steps down to the cellar.

Lawrs went to the cellar first. It had a dirt floor and an old coal-burning furnace with pipes running up to the house from the plenum. There was a coal bin against one wall. A chute ran down to it from a small opening in the foundation; an iron, hinged door gave access to the chute from the outside. It reminded Lawrs of when he was young, and his dad sent him down to shovel coal into their furnace. Lucky for him, in the late forties, his dad added a stoker with an auger to feed the coal into the fire. All the neighbors were envious: it had a thermostat to activate the stoker, and all you had to do was empty the ash pan. There weren't even any big clinkers.

Most farmers had concrete floors in their cellars so that they stayed cleaner. That was necessary because they separated the cream from the milk down there. They would use a large metal tank to store the cans of milk and cream in cool water until the creamery picked them up. The woman of the house would have long wooden shelves of canned fruit, tomatoes, beans, applesauce, pickles, and other foods from her garden; she would also keep flats of eggs in the basement until she took them to town to sell on Saturday.

Lawrs went up the stairs to the main floor where a door opened into a small hall that separated the dining and living rooms.

Truesdale's dining room contained a veneered oak table and a few mismatched chairs; the veneer was beginning to peel off the table. The floor appeared to be maple, but had not been taken care of.

The kitchen was at the back; the floor was covered by a dirty, cracked linoleum. There were even dirty dishes in the sink and a mess on the little table where Truesdale must have eaten his meals. The stove hadn't been cleaned recently. It had four propane burners on one side and a wood stove on the other side. Typically, the wood stove wasn't used to cook; people burnt old newspapers and garbage in it, or they used it to heat the kitchen in the winter.

The living room ran across the full front of the house. The floors were like the ones in the dining room. There was no rug. There was, however, a large bloodstain on the floor; undoubtedly, that was the place where Truesdale had been shot. Lawrs' stomach didn't get upset easily, but the smell was putrid, especially in the heat. He choked. The only other things in the room were a worn couch and a beat-up upholstered chair that no one would want to sit on. There was no television set, and as far as Lawrs could see, not even a radio. No wonder this guy was mad at the world. He didn't go upstairs.

He could imagine what he would find up there, and it wouldn't be good.

Lawrs exited through the back door in the kitchen. From an uncovered porch, stairs led down to the yard.

Just beyond a fence that had fallen down in several places, there was a tool shed and a chicken coop. As he walked down the stairs, the dog started to bark again. Lawrs saw the can where Jim said there would be dog food; there was an old scoop inside. Lawrs used it to take some food to the dog. "Dog, how ya doing? It'll be okay. See, I brought some food." As he got closer, the dog stopped barking and started to wag his tail. With his free hand, Lawrs reached out to pat his head. The dog wasn't afraid. Lawrs put the food in his pan; the dog hungrily started to eat.

Lawrs could see a small opening on one side of the coop; the chickens used it to get to the dirt area where they were fed and looked for bugs; some farmers just threw their food on the ground. There was a hinged flap over the door to shut the chickens inside the coop at night; it was intended to protect them from raccoons, skunks, and other predators. The chicken wire surrounding the outdoor area was very high, but now there were large holes in it.

The door to the coop didn't move easily. He had to pull hard just to get it about half open. It was about to fall off. Standing in the doorway, he could see the place was in shambles. One of the rows of wooden boxes attached to the wall, where the hens would have laid their eggs, had fallen to the ground on one end. The roof obviously leaked.

If he bought the place, Lawrs thought, he'd just tear the place down and burn the wood. It wouldn't be good for anything else.

Suddenly, he became aware of a very strong, unpleasant odor. It made him gag, just like the smell in the living room. He pulled out his handkerchief and put it over his nose.

It was dark in the chicken coop, but as his eyes adjusted, he saw what he thought was a large sack in the far corner. He couldn't imagine what it was. He walked over to it. He used the dog scoop he still had in his hand to push it. It fell over. It wasn't a sack. It was a man's body.

Suddenly there was a loud squeak. The door behind him had been opened farther. Was it Truesdale's killer?

A deep voice said, "Who's there?"

Lawrs turned around. It was Bob Rath, Truesdale's part-time hired hand.

"Bob, it's Lawrs. Look!" He pointed to the body.

"God! A body. Who is it?"

"I can't tell. We have to call the sheriff. Is there a phone in the house?"

"No. Ross has one. Oh, God. This place is jinxed."

Lawrs said, "I'll go over to Jim's."

"I'm coming with you," Rath said quickly.

The two men hurried out and walked across the road.

Jim wasn't in the barn where he had been when Lawrs had talked to him earlier, so he knocked on the back door of the house.

Shirley, Jim's wife, came to the door.

"Lawrs. Bob. What's going on? Can I help you? Jim's out in the feed lot," she said, pointing out behind the barn.

"Shirley, we need to use your phone. There's no easy way to put it, but there's a body in Truesdale's chicken coop!"

"Oh, heavens! Not another body! Who's is it?"

"I don't know. It's in bad shape. I have to call the sheriff."

"Of course. It's in the dining room." She walked into the dining room, pointed at the phone, and stepped back. "It's a party-line; you'll have to ring the operator. Her name is Jane."

Lawrs stood in front of the phone; it was about chest high on the wall. The mouthpiece angled down toward his face; it could be adjusted higher or lower. He took the earpiece off the hook with his left hand; he used his right one to crank the handle that rang the bell. He gave it one long, single ring. On a party line, that was how you alerted the telephone operator. On small, rural exchanges the switchboard was sometimes located in the operator's home.

Jane answered right away. "Operator. Can I help you?"

When you rang in on a party line, the operator couldn't tell who was calling, so you had to identify yourself. "Jane, this is Lawrs Jensen. I'm at Jim Ross' place. We've found another body at Truesdale's. Call the sheriff. Don't connect me; just tell him to get over here, quick as he can. Have him bring the coroner and something to take the body away in. Maybe you should call the Belle Plaine chief of police, too."

On a party line, you always knew someone could listen in. Someone was listening as Lawrs talked to the operator. She spoke up without identifying herself. "What's happened? Where's the body? Who is it?"

Lawrs didn't know the person, so he just said, "Lady, it's in the chicken coop." Re-addressing the operator, he said, "Jane, just get the sheriff!"

"I sure will," Jane said as she disconnected herself.

The neighbor waited only a few moments after she hung up; then she rang the line—one long and three shorts. That was the signal that there was an emergency such as a fire or a tornado; everyone was expected to pick up. After waiting for a significant number of people to join the call, the neighbor told them what she had just heard. When she finished, she called WMT. Fifteen minutes later, anyone with a radio on could hear:

"We interrupt this regularly scheduled broadcast to announce late-breaking news. An informant has told WMT that a second body has been discovered on the farm of John Truesdale, the man who was found shot to death last Wednesday near Blairstown. A neighbor found the body. The name of the dead man is not known. We have not been able to contact the sheriff's office yet, but stay tuned for additonal news. We will interrupt our regularly scheduled programs as we have additional information."

Jim had come into the dining room just as Lawrs was explaining to the operator what he had found at Truesdale's. As he stood, waiting for Lawrs to finish, he put his arm around Shirley; he knew she was upset.

Lawrs and Bob remained at Jim's house. After they speculated for a while about the identity of the body and the murderer, Jim said, "I'll go over and get the dog. He'll go crazy when the sheriff shows up. He knows me; I'm sure he'll come."

Ten minutes passed as Bob, Shirley, and Lawrs talked about what had happened. As Jim came back in from getting the dog, they heard a siren. Belle Plaine's police chief, Harvey Park, pulled into Truesdale's driveway. Technically, because the incident had occurred in the county, it was not in Park's jurisdiction. But, Lawrs had asked the operator to call him because he was only a few minutes away, whereas it would take the sheriff at least fifteen or twenty minutes to get there.

THE THREE MEN WALKED ACROSS the road to Park's car. Shirley didn't go with them; the kids would be coming home on the school bus soon, and she didn't want them to find their home empty, especially with police vehicles across the road again.

Park got out of his car; Lawrs quickly filled him in.

Park wanted all three men to stay until the sheriff arrived. "I called the sheriff just before I left the station. He already knew; the operator called him. Wait here; I'll go in and look around."

After what seemed an eternity, but was probably only three or four minutes, Park came out. "I don't recognize him. The body's in bad shape. It' been there several days; in this heat it's really deteriorated."

Fifteen minutes later, the sheriff showed up. An old hearse being used as a coroner's van was behind him; the coroner, a retired doctor, was driving it. The four men went over to the sheriff's car.

Even before they could tell him what they had found, the sheriff got out of the car yelling, "Who the hell called WMT? I heard you found a body on the radio before I could even get here. Which one of you called them?"

The men just looked at each other. "We didn't do it, sheriff," Lawrs said. "I just called you and chief Park; somebody must have listened in on the party line."

"You'd better not have called them," the sheriff shouted, "otherwise, I'll have you up on a charge of interfering with a police investigation!"

"Look, sheriff, we didn't do it," Lawrs said firmly. "Do you want to know what we found or don't you?"

Lawrs told him quickly what he had discovered and where, pointing to the chicken coop.

"Did you touch the body?" the sheriff asked accusingly.

"No, of course not. Who'd want to?" Lawrs said.

After he was through talking to the three men, the sheriff and the coroner went into the chicken coop, followed by Park.

Lawrs, Jim, and Bob all went back to Jim's yard. Shirley came out. They told her the sheriff was upset about someone calling WMT.

"Odds on, it was Mary Jarvis," Shirley said. "She's the one who listens in the most; she's a real gossip." However, they weren't about to get her in trouble by telling the sheriff.

After looking at the body for whatever evidence remained, the sheriff, the coroner, and the chief came out of the coop; they were holding handkerchiefs over their noses. The coroner went to get his stretcher. He and chief Park, both with gloves on, went in to bring the body out.

The sheriff motioned Lawrs, Jim, Shirley, and Bob to come over.

After the body had been brought out and they all were assembled, he pulled back the sheet the coroner had placed over the body. "Do any of you recognize him?"

Shirley started to slump; her husband held her up. Everyone looked at the gruesome sight. There was a wound directly on the corpse's forehead. He obviously had been shot. The body was swollen, and the smell was awful. They all said they didn't know the person. Shirley turned her face to Jim's chest; Lawrs could tell she was trying hard not to cry.

The sheriff directed the coroner and Park to put the body in the old hearse.

As the men continued to talk, the school bus drove up, stopped, and let the two Ross children out. Ross and Shirley went over to walk them to the house. Jim picked up his daughter and was talking with her. Shirley had Tim by the hand. Thankfully, the coroner and Park had gotten the body into the hearse just before the school bus stopped.

The sheriff told Lawrs he could leave, but he might need him later.

Then the sheriff, the coroner, and the chief went into Truesdale's house; they wanted to look for other evidence. Bob Rath went to feed the cattle.

Lawrs drove home, in a state of disbelief. Who had been killed? Why? Who was the murderer?

Chapter Seven

Thursday Morning, August 28, 1953

There was a great deal of new information for The Rounders to process the next morning.

"I can't believe there's another body," Stoner said. "Lawrs, you found it?"

"Yes, in the chicken coop of all places. It was in really bad condition." Lawrs went on to tell them how he had visited Jim Ross and subsequently discovered the man's body.

"Has anyone identified it?" Roy asked.

"No, I don't think so," Lawrs answered.

"Who do they think did it?"

Lawrs offered: "I don't know. I'm guessing they think the person who killed Truesdale also killed the second guy. They're still looking for the uncle. He's probably the leading suspect."

Roy then asked, "Pansy, did the sheriff ever call you about the uncle's visit to your garage? I told him that you could identify the pickup."

"Of course he didn't. You could put a dead mouse under his nose, and he wouldn't smell it."

"Except, maybe, a dead body that had been out in the heat for several days," Lawrs said, half seriously, half humorously.

At that point, Sam Winfield came in with Mac's mail. He knew about the second body; a postman heard everything. He was a quiet man, however, and seldom gossiped with people on his route. He was, as Lawrs' speech teacher at Iowa State would have said, an active listener. Mac invited him to sit in on the discussion. He repeated what he had said before: he couldn't stay long; if he did, the customers at the end of his route would complain. Nonetheless, he stayed. Mac asked Lawrs to repeat the story about finding the body for his benefit.

When Lawrs finished, they went back to the discussion of the break-in at Dot's. Pansy told the group that he had visited Dot's neighbor. He explained that Mac had asked him to find out if she could identify the pickup she saw at the time of the robbery. They both wanted to know if her description matched that of Truesdale's uncle's truck. To help her, Pansy had torn a page out of one of his automotive magazines; it was a picture of the same model and year as Truesdale's uncle's pickup. In the picture, however, the truck was green, not dark blue. "The fact that the color was different seemed to throw her off although she said the two pickups looked alike. I asked her about the color of the license plate. She didn't think it was an Iowa plate, but when I asked her if it was black, like Ohio plates, she didn't know."

Addressing Pansy, Mac said. "It would've been nice if she'd known for sure, but I appreciate you going over. You know cars and trucks better than anybody else."

The Rounders discussed whether the two pickups were the same; the consensus was that they could have been, but they could think of no reason why the uncle would have robbed Dot.

Stoner told them that Mac had bought a walnut box at Dot's. "Listen to this," she said dramatically. "An old Ohio county history in the box showed the name Truesdale." With great emphasis, she added, "Dot purchased it in Ohio—where Truesdale's uncle came from. Show them where it is, Mac."

Mac pointed to the box on a table in the middle of the room; everyone turned to look.

"That is interesting," Sam said, entering into the discussion for the first time. "Was John Truesdale mentioned?"

"No, it was published in 1873—far too early to have included him."

"Was the name Caldwell in it?" Roy asked. "I found out at the courthouse that before Truesdale owned the property, it belonged to his mother. Her maiden name was Sarah Caldwell. She had inherited it from her parents. Their names were Joseph and Marie Caldwell."

Mac responded. "I didn't know to look."

Sam offered, "I'll go look." He got up, went to the box, and thumbed through the history. He returned to the table, saying that he couldn't find a main entry for a Caldwell.

"Is there anything else in the box?" Roy asked.

Mac answered, "There was a handwritten genealogy in an old bible; it had some Truesdales, but they were too early to include John. There was an inventory for an Edward Truesdale's estate, and," she added, "some old family pictures."

"By the way," Roy said, "when I looked up Truesdale's property, I found he had three liens on it—so he probably didn't have any equity in it."

Everyone was quiet for a few moments. Then, Fritz made a suggestion. "Maybe whoever killed Truesdale was seen by his uncle, so the killer had to kill him, too. That could explain why there were two bodies, and it would mean that the second body is the uncle."

Several people said that seemed plausible.

Stoner loved to be dramatic; it was time for her bombshell. She held out both hands as though she was quieting a crowd. "I think Old Man Martinek killed Truesdale. Remember? Lawrs mentioned that Truesdale had dated Martinek's daughter. He said that she was pregnant, maybe by Truesdale." She paused for dramatic effect. "Well, it's true! I went over to the Happy Farmer where Shelia works. She's not only five or six months along, she said Truesdale was the father. And—" she paused, spacing each word for effect, "She said her dad killed Truesdale!"

Her intention was to shock her audience, and she succeeded. Her information startled everyone, except Fritz, with whom she'd told previously. —Somewhat against his better judgment, he had agreed not to tell the other Rounders what she had told him until she brought it up.

"Martinek!" said Pansy. "Why've you been holding out on us, Stoner?"

"To be fair," Stoner said, somewhat more cautiously, "Shelia told me that after Martinek found out Truesdale was dead, he said something like 'somebody beat me to it.'"

"He probably was just covering himself," Pansy said.

"Absolutely," Stoner agreed.

Roy, always the skeptical lawyer, said, "Let's not jump to conclusions. We'll just have to wait and see if the sheriff confirms that it's the uncle."

Stoner offered, in a tone slightly less bombastic than her earlier announcement, "For sure, Martinek is capable of it. He's a piece of work. He's shouted at me several times over the stupidest things, and when he threw Shelia out, he called her a word—well, I won't say the word, but it rhymes with 'floor.'"

"Did you tell the sheriff?" Fritz asked.

"I always do what you tell me to do, Fritz," Stoner said, trying to sound subservient, but not pulling it off. "The sheriff said he'd look into it, but I have my doubts. You know what I think of him."

It was eleven thirty and Lawrs figured that their discussion was about at an end. "Pansy, did you hear the one about the old farmer?"

"It better be a clean one, Lawrs," Mac said, accepting the inevitable.

"Oh, it is," Lawrs rejoined. "Well, Homer and his wife were leaning against the their pig pen when she remembered that their golden wedding anniversary was the next week. 'We'll have a party,' she said; 'we'll slaughter a pig.' Homer scratched his head. 'Gee, Ethel,' he finally said, 'I don't see why a pig should take the blame for something that happened fifty years ago.'"

There were a few guffaws.

As they were getting up to leave, Sam Winfield thanked them for letting him sit in on their discussion.

"You'll just have to join us every week," Mac said.

"I'd like that," he said, "but it doesn't work with my schedule. I'll stop in when I can."

"Well, the invitation is there," Mac said.

"Thanks, again."

As they left, Fritz and Sam went past the box Mac had bought at Dot's. They both rummaged through it for a while, and then left.

Lawrs didn't leave; as he usually did, he went to the counter to have lunch. Roy, who had hung back as the rest of the people left, said to him, "Lawrs, I need to ask something. Jim Ross referred Bill Robinson to me for some legal help. I think you said you knew him."

"I do, but I've only met him a couple of times. He isn't a good friend or anything."

"He told me there is a ravine between his property and Truesdale's."

"That's right. When I was over there, I could see it out beyond his farrowing sheds."

"Robinson says that the property line doesn't conform to the ravine. He says he owns a piece of land across the ravine from his place, next to Truesdale's land. Right now it's not fenced off, but he'd like to fence it for grazing."

Roy continued, "When he told Truesdale what he was going to do, he said Truesdale acted like a crazy man. He even pointed a gun at him. He said that he had to get his own gun to get him to leave."

"Didn't Fritz say Truesdale had gotten into a fight with Robinson at Kelley's a while back?" Lawrs asked.

"Yes," Roy replied, "maybe that's what the fight was about."

Lawrs agreed, "I guess everyone has had trouble with Truesdale, even Stoner has had trouble with him. Jim Ross said the only way he got along with him was to stay clear of him."

Roy continued, "Robinson wants me to confirm the property lines. He wants to protect his rights if Robinson's heirs sell the place. I told him that I would go to Vinton and check. I just wanted to ask if you know Robinson; I don't want to get cross-wise with some crazy man."

Lawrs replied, "I don't know anything that should be a red flag, but I'll ask Jim next time I see him."

"Thanks," Roy said, "I'd appreciate that." He left to catch a ride home with Pansy who had been waiting in his truck impatiently. Roy always rode to Rounders' meetings with Pansy.

Lawrs stayed for lunch as Ruthie hoped he would. She asked him what he wanted. He told her 'the usual.' That meant a loose meat sandwich and a grape Nehi. Mac couldn't call them Maid-Rites because she would not pay to use the trademarked name. People liked them and talked as if they were gourmet items. Mac's trick was that after she cooked the meat, drained off the fat, and rinsed it, she would add her secret ingredients: vinegar and some special spices.

Ruthie had a plan about how she would get Lawrs attention this morning; she would use compliments. "Lawrs, you were so brave when you found that body. I would have fallen apart."

"I wasn't really brave. When I found it, I almost gagged from the smell."

"Yes, but it must have been hard to do. Was the body all bloody and everything?" she asked.

"Not exactly, just a bullet hole in his head; that's all."

"Oh, how awful, and, I don't care what you say, you were brave."

"Thanks."

"What are you going to do now?"

"What do you mean?"

"Well, now that you've found the body, how will you find out who it was?"

"That's not my job. That's the sheriff's job."

He started to eat his loose-meat sandwich and listen to the noon market reports from Chicago; he asked her to turn the radio up.

She was crestfallen.

Chapter Eight

Saturday, August 30, 1952

Lawrs was still thinking about the body. He had a few nightmares about it. Who was it? It could be the person who killed Truesdale. If so, who killed him? Of course, it could be the other way around: Truesdale killed him and put the body out in the chicken coop. If that was the case, then who killed Truesdale? Maybe Fritz was right: Martinek killed them both.

He told himself to stop worrying about it.

He didn't usually get hung up on something. He tended not to see problems when there weren't any. When there was a problem, he got on with solving it. For example, in college, he'd tried out for the football team but didn't make it; he wasn't heavy enough. He didn't dwell on the loss. He tried out for track and got on the team as a sprinter. He wasn't the best sprinter around, but he held up his end and occasionally won.

Of course, when Lawrs' parents had both been killed in an accident late one afternoon in 1946, when he was twenty-two, he was devastated and couldn't get what had happened out of his head. After several months of being depressed, he decided he had to get on with it. Now, the only time the memory came back fresh in his mind was when he was driving west on the Lincoln Highway in the late afternoon, and the sun was in his eyes. The highway patrol thought his father had probably been looking into the sun and was temporarily blinded, causing him to lose control and crash head-on into another car. At least they died instantly, and the man in the other car eventually recovered.

His parents had left him a good farm. The land was flat and fertile. It always produced well, and, because he'd gone to ag school, he knew what to do to increase productivity.

He had already expanded the farm once. He had bought a small property next to his own when it came up for sale. He was thinking about expanding again. None of the land that was adjacent to his property was currently for sale, but the property didn't have to be close; he would let someone else manage it and just collect rent in the form of a share of the crops. That's why he was looking at Truesdale's farm.

ABOUT NINE-THIRTY IN THE MORNING, Lawrs got a call from Jim Ross. He remembered that Lawrs was interested in Truesdale's farm, and he had asked him to keep an eye out for his relatives.

Jim called to tell Lawrs that Truesdale's cousins from Ohio had arrived; he had gone over and introduced himself.

Lawrs decided he would drive over there and talk with them.

While he was driving there, he had the radio tuned to WMT. It was hard to believe, but they broke into the programming, again—as they had when Truesdale was found, and when he had discovered the second body. Now, a third time. Heaven help us, he thought, not another murder; the community can't take another one.

The announcer was talking, "We have learned from the sheriff's office in Vinton this morning that the second body found on the John Truesdale farm has been identified. The body was that of

Truesdale's uncle, Earnest Caldwell from Ohio. Relatives from Ohio came to Benton County to identify his body at the request of county sheriff, Ralph Kretzler. The sheriff has indicated Mr. Caldwell was shot in the head, probably with a handgun. We hope to have additional information on this story on the noon news. Please stay tuned to WMT. We now take you back to the regularly scheduled broadcast."

The first thing that came to Lawrs' mind was that at least Sheriff Kretzler had been able to control the news this time; the information hadn't been leaked by a nosy neighbor on a party line.

Truesdale's uncle. That made sense to Lawrs. If the uncle had seen Martinek kill Truesdale, then he would have to kill the uncle to keep him quiet.

But the stories didn't line up. Why would he have been found in the chicken coop when Truesdale was killed in the house? Then, there was the problem of the guns: Truesdale had been killed by a shotgun blast, but the uncle was killed with a handgun. It still didn't quite make sense.

And, where was the uncle's truck? The only explanation was that the killer had driven it off, but if that were true, where was the killer's car? Surely he wouldn't have walked back to the farm to get it. And what had this all to do with the robbery at Dot's? Still too many questions and not enough answers, Lawrs thought.

When he got to Truesdale's farm, there was a black 1952 Dodge Coronet in the yard with black Ohio license plates. The side door of the house was open although the screen was closed.

"Hello, anybody here?" Lawrs called out as he pulled the screen door open and stuck his head inside. No one answered, so he knocked, and called a little louder, "Hello, is there anyone here?"

A man came down to the side door from the first floor. Lawrs could see the physical resemblance to Truesdale. He was tall and lanky.

"Sorry," Lawrs said, "I don't mean to bother you. My name is

Lawrence Jensen. I go by Lawrs. I live over near Newhall. I'm really sorry about John. His death shocked everybody around here."

Lawrs reached out to shake the man's hand, and he accepted it firmly. "Thanks, I'm Harold Caldwell."

"I just heard on the radio that the sheriff has identified the second body. Was it your father?"

"Yes, it was."

"Oh, I am so very sorry. I shouldn't have come, but when I started out, I didn't know they'd identified him."

"That's all right," Caldwell said, "When we knew he was missing, and when a second body had been found, we assumed it was him. The sheriff called and asked us to come over and identify the body. We went over to Vinton late yesterday."

"I was the one who discovered him."

"Oh, the sheriff told me that a young man had found it. It must have been awful, the body was so deteriorated; it was hard for us to look at it."

"The neighbor across the road, Jim Ross, told me that you were here. I came over because I wanted to talk to you about the farm. I assume you know that a man named Bob Rath has been coming in every day to take care of things?"

"Yes, we met him this morning."

"That's good. We were all worried about him. He'd been coming out of loyalty to John. But he wasn't being paid. I wanted to be sure you knew."

"Yes, he told us. We've made arrangements to cover what he's owed. He's agreed to keep coming 'til we can settle things."

"That's great. I don't want to seem pushy, but we're also concerned about the corn crop. It's going to have to be picked in the next few weeks, and I don't think there's a corn picker on the farm. Several of us are willing to help, but we were uncomfortable doing it until we could check with you."

"Oh, I'm sorry. We didn't know that, and Bob didn't mention it. I run a hardware store in Ohio, and I don't know much about farming. We'd certainly appreciate any help you can arrange."

"Let me see what we can do; I'll get back to you," Lawrs said. Continuing, he asked, "Have you decided what you will do with the place?"

"No, honestly, this has all happened so fast, we just haven't had time to think."

"This probably isn't a good time to ask, but would you consider selling? Even before this happened, I've been looking for a place where I could expand."

"Macy," Caldwell called back into the house. "There's somebody here who's interested in buying the place." A woman appeared on the landing above the two men. She had obviously been cleaning. "This is my wife, Macy. Macy, this is Lawrs Jensen, he lives around here."

"Yes, I live over by Newhall," Lawrs said. "It isn't too far from here. I'm so sorry for your loss."

She was considerably shorter than her husband and was heavy without being fat. She had a broad smile on her face. She was the kind of Midwest woman who was always cheery and willing to help out. She came down the steps and offered her hand.

"I was just telling your husband that I heard about his father on the radio as I was coming over. If I'd known, I wouldn't have come. I hate to bother you at a time like this."

"He's the one who found dad, Macy."

"Oh, dear, how awful for you. We were afraid something like this had happened when we heard John had been killed, and Harold's father was missing."

"Yes, that's what your husband said," Lawrs responded.

"Come on in," Mrs. Caldwell offered.

They walked up the short flight of stairs to the main floor of the house. Mrs. Caldwell continued talking, "This place is a mess; there isn't even a good place to sit down—certainly not in the living room. I've been trying to clean up the blood in there, and the flies are terrible. Let's go into the dining room, at least there are some clean chairs in there." As they walked into the dining room, it was obvious to Lawrs that things had been cleaned up. They all sat down.

"Macy, he came to be sure we knew that Bob Rath hadn't been paid. He also mentioned the corn crop needs to be harvested soon. He said some neighbors might help out. I told him we aren't farmers."

Caldwell's wife said, "No, we aren't. Harold and his brother run a hardware store their father started. It's in Marietta, Ohio, southeast of Columbus, right across the river from West Virginia."

"I can really understand the pain you must be going through," Lawrs said to the couple. "I know how hard it is to suddently find out something like this. My parents died in an auto accident a few years ago, and I got a call to come and identify the bodies," Lawrs said.

"Oh, I'm so sorry," Macy responded.

"I don't want to bother you," Lawrs continued. "I'm sure you have a lot to do to clear things up. I just came by because I wanted to know if you'd be interested in renting or selling the place. I know this isn't the right time to think about that, but if you are interested, I'd like to talk with you later."

Harold responded, "It is just a little early to decide what to do. My brother and I have no interest in it. But I need to get back to Ohio to see what he does want to do. Whatever it is, we need to make the decision together."

"I understand," Lawrs said. "Are you planning on staying here tonight?"

Macy answered quickly, "Oh, no. It's just not in good shape, and we wouldn't want to stay in the place where they were both were killed."

Caldwell said, "We took a motel room in Vinton yesterday. We'll go back there tonight."

Lawrs thanked them, shook their hands, and left.

BEFORE HE WENT BACK TO his place, he decided to go across the road and talk with Jim Ross again. He wanted to discover additional information about Bill Robinson, the man who had asked Roy to look into the property line issue at the back of Truesdale's farm.

It was Saturday, and Jim and his family might be in town; most farmers did go to town on Saturdays to buy their supplies, sell their eggs, park on Main Street, and watch everyone else go by. Saturday night in any Midwest town was a time when everyone either drove around or sat and watched everyone else drive around.

Lawrs was lucky, however; Jim, his wife, and their children were there. They had just finished lunch and were sitting at the kitchen table. When Lawrs knocked, Jim came to the door.

"Hi, Lawrs," he said. "Did you meet Truesdale's relatives?"

"Yes, thanks for calling. Did you know they identified the second body as Truesdale's uncle?"

"I didn't know it when I called you, but Shirley heard it on the radio this morning. It must be awful for them. We plan to ask them over here for supper."

"I'm sure they'd really appreciate that. —Jim, do you have a minute? I need to ask you something."

"Let's go into the living room."

As they sat down, Jim asked Lawrs if he had asked if the Caldwell's were interested in selling the farm. He also asked if they knew how they'd get the corn in.

Lawrs told him about Harold's brother back in Ohio, and how he would have to be consulted before they could make any decisions about the property. Lawrs also told him they had paid Bob Rath and asked him to stay on until they worked something out. That pleased Jim; it took a possible load off his back. They talked briefly about getting several neighbors and their corn pickers together to harvest the crop when the time came. Jim asked Lawrs if he had remembered to talk to Roy about any liability they might incur if they got involved in harvesting the corn.

"Sorry, I forgot to ask," he said, "but Roy was the reason I came over. He told me that you recommended that Bill Robinson talk to him about the property line between their farms."

"Yes," Jim said, "he has questions about it. He's been trying to fence off some of his land on Truesdale's side of the ravine. Truesdale was giving him a hard time; he claimed he owned the land out to the edge of the ravine."

Lawrs asked, "What's Robinson like? I told Roy I would ask you. With all the strange stuff going on, he didn't want to get involved with a trouble maker."

"Well, I don't know too much. He's got a wife and a couple of kids. He's a good farmer, and he keeps his place in good shape. He and Truesdale had some bad disagreements, but I don't think Robinson started most of them."

"Most of them? Roy only talked about one fight—when Truesdale threatened him if he put up a fence."

"They had several fights that I know of. Once, one of Robinson's steers got onto Truesdale's place. Then, Truesdale said Robinson was burning brush too close to his property; he thought the fire would spread to his place. Another time, they argued because Robinson was planting experimental seed corn; Truesdale said the pollen was drifting over to his place and would alter his crop—which, of course, is nonsense."

Jim continued, "It was almost always Truesdale who started the arguments, but Robinson gave as good as he got. You've met him; he's a big guy, and I wouldn't want him to meet him in a dark alley. The only fight I know that Robinson started was when Truesdale's dog got loose and killed one of Robinson's chickens, or so he claimed."

"'Dog?' That nice dog tied up in the yard, the one you brought back over here? He didn't seem to me like that kind of a dog. What's going to happen to him anyway?"

"No, it's not the same dog. It was one that Truesdale had before he got the one you saw. We're going to keep him unless the Caldwell's want him; the kids enjoy playing with him, and he is very gentle."

Going back to the discussion about Truesdale, Lawrs said, "Well, I'm sure I'm not telling you anything new, but, there was bad blood between Truesdale and lots of other folks. Have you heard Old Man Martinek threatened him because he thought he'd gotten his daughter pregnant?"

"Yes, everyone is talking about that," Jim said. "I wonder now if it was Martinek that Truesdale had the big argument with."

"Could've been. But, Robinson could have done it—maybe in an argument over the fence."

"I wouldn't want to think he'd do something like that," Jim said, "but given all the stuff going on around here, anything is possible. It just seems to me that it's more likely that Martinek did it."

When they had finished talking, they went through to the kitchen where Shirley was washing dishes. They talked for a while, but not at all about the killings because Ross's children were sitting at the table doing their homework.

Lawrs left and returned home. He felt some closure now that the second body had been identified. There was also something comforting about having met the Caldwells; there were nice people. It was unfortunate, he thought, that Truesdale hadn't gotten more of the family genes. Finally, the case seemed closer to being solved; it had to be Martinek or Robinson. —But, then, there was still the problem of the guns and the car.

Chapter Nine

Tuesday, September 2, 1952

About two o'clock Clyde Martinek came into Pansy's garage. It was hot, and Pansy had the garage door open. Martinek drove his pickup directly inside without asking Pansy first. Pansy put his *Chicago Tribune* down and went to the doorway between the office and the garage.

"Hello, Clyde. What can I do for you?"

Pointing at his truck, he said, "This damned thing keeps stalling on me. I replaced the filter, but that didn't work, so I took it over to the dealer. They couldn't fix it, and to top it off, they charged me four bucks. They're not getting my business again."

"Well, let me have a look at it. Come back around four-thirty and I'll tell you what I know."

"What are you going to charge me?" he demanded.

"I won't charge you anything if I can't fix it, but if I can, I'll charge you parts and labor."

"What's your labor cost?"

"Two dollars an hour."

"Two dollars! Hell, minimum wage isn't a dollar."

"Sorry, I don't work at minimum wage. Take it or leave it."

Martinek growled, "I guess I don't have no damn choice. I'll go to Kelley's and be back at four-thirty. But don't you siphon off any gas; it's up to twenty cents a gallon."

"Four-thirty," Pansy said again. "I'll have it fixed by then, or at least I'll have it so you can drive it."

Pansy did not like to do routine automotive maintenance such as changing the oil, tuning up cars, fixing flat tires, or anything that filling stations do. He was only interested in unusual problems; he had been known to go out to a farmer's field to fix a combine no one else could get to work. But, in this situation, he wanted to humor Martinek in order to find out how he might be connected to Truesdale's killing. He decided to wait and talk to him when he came back to get the truck.

Martinek stalked off. He went to Kelley's tavern three blocks away. When he got there, he sat by himself and didn't say anything to the other patrons. When Kelley asked how he was, he didn't answer. He just said he wanted a Pabst draft. He drank five of them in the next two and a half hours.

By the time he got back to Pansy's, he wasn't steady on his feet, and his speech was slurred.

Pansy knew the signs.

"Well, did ya get the damn thing done? What was it?" He demanded.

Pansy calmly told him that the carburetor just needed some adjustments.

"Why the hell couldn't the dealer figure that out?"

"I don't know."

"How much?"

"Two dollars. It just took me about an hour, and there were no parts involved," Pansy said quietly.

"That's robbery!" However, he took his wallet out and gave Pansy two dollars.

Pansy didn't expect to hear a thank you; he wanted to see what he could tease out of Martinek about Truesdale.

"How's your daughter, Clyde? I understand you're going to be a grandfather."

"That bitch. I threw her out. I don't want anything to do with her, her baby, or her damn lover."

As nicely as he could, Pansy said. "Oh, I'm sorry to hear that Clyde. I haven't heard who she was engaged to."

"She wasn't damned engaged," he shouted. "It was that devil, Truesdale. All I can say is he got what he deserved."

"Don't say that, Clyde. You don't mean that."

"Don't assume nothing!" Martinek responded. "I'll just say it again: he got what he deserved, and I'm damned glad he's dead. He deserved to have his head blown off. And that's all I'll say."

Martinek turned and stormed out of Pansy's office, getting into his truck, turning the motor over easily, and backing out rapidly. He didn't look behind him as he pulled out; he backed into on-coming traffic, made a tight turn on the street, and took off fast.

Pansy was disturbed. Not only did Martinek put others at risk the way he backed out of the garage and drove off, but it also sounded as if he might have killed Truesdale. He decided he would call the sheriff and tell him what he said.

The sheriff had gone home by the time Pansy got someone to answer the phone at his office. It was his deputy. "Walt, this is Frank O'Malley over at my garage in Belle Plaine. I want to tell the sheriff something important, but if he isn't in, I'll tell you."

"Go ahead, Frank. I'll be sure he gets the message."

"Clyde Martinek was over here this afternoon. He wanted me to work on his truck. I got it fixed, but before he left, he really sounded off about Truesdale. I won't repeat his cuss words, but he said he was glad he was dead, and he said he had it coming. He also said

Truesdale had gotten his daughter pregnant. He was serious. The sheriff needs to look into it."

"Thanks for calling," the deputy said. "I'll be sure the sheriff hears about it. He'll want to call you—he might even come over. Will you be there tomorrow?"

"I'm here every day including Saturday. But, I take Wednesday afternoon and Sundays off. If he wants to talk to me tomorrow afternoon, call me at home, and I'll be glad to come down and talk to him."

Pansy added, "While he was waiting on his truck, he went over to Kelley's and downed quite a few. He drove out of here like a steer that's just had his you-know-whats cut off. He's not safe to be on the road. You might also want to talk to Kelley to see if he said anything else about Truesdale over there."

"We'll sure follow up, Pansy. Thanks again for letting us know." The deputy hung up.

Pansy was pretty steamed up. He'd kept his tongue in check when he was talking with Martinek, but now he was mad. He dropped down into his office chair and pulled out the lower drawer where he kept some whiskey. He poured a small glass and downed it in one gulp. He started out for home right away. He didn't want to be unsafe on the road himself, but he knew he could get there before the effects of the drink caught up with him; his house was only six blocks from his garage.

As soon as he hung up, Deputy Mosley called the sheriff. He got him at his home having an early supper with his wife. He knew that Stoner had called to tell the sheriff what Shelia Martinek had told her, but Mosley also knew that the sheriff had done nothing as a result of her call. He hadn't even checked with Pansy about the fact that he had fixed Truesdale's uncle's pickup. He knew the sheriff had a poor track record for getting things done.

Mosley told him what Pansy had said, including the fact that

Martinek was drunk. He suggested that the sheriff should call Pansy tomorrow and, possibly, he might want to talk to Kelley at his tavern in Belle Plaine. The sheriff said decidedly, "No, I'll just go see Martinek tomorrow. Be ready! And," he added, "call chief Park; let him know about Martinek being drunk."

Chapter Ten

Wednesday, September 3, 1952

The next day was cooler and cloudy. August seemed to be behind them, and the smell of burning leaves was in the air. About nine o'clock, the sheriff and his deputy drove to the Martinek farm south of Belle Plaine. It took about thirty-five minutes from Vinton. It was bottom land that was fertile when the weather was right, but it flooded when the Iowa River was out of its banks—usually every four or five years.

The sheriff knew Martinek was home because his pickup was parked along the side of the house. He told his deputy to wait in the yard and have his gun out. The sheriff walked onto the porch. The window shade was down, but, as he approached, someone pulled it far enough away from the window to peer out. It wasn't a good sign.

The sheriff knocked on the door. "It's Sheriff Kretzler. I need to speak with you." No one replied. He knocked again, a little harder. "This is Sheriff Kretzler, Martinek, I want to talk with you."

"I know damned well what you want to talk about," Martinek replied, yelling through the door. "I don't have a damned thing to say."

"That won't do, Clyde." The sheriff said firmly. "Come out, or I'll have to come in, and that won't be good for either one of us." The sheriff could tell he had been drinking.

Suddenly the door opened with a bang as it swung back against the inside wall. Clyde was standing in the doorway with his shotgun pointed at the sheriff.

"I'm tellin' ya," Martinek yelled, "I don't have nothin' to say to you." He looked over the sheriff's shoulder and said loudly, "Just take that deputy and get off my property. Now!"

The sheriff retained his composure. "Look," he said, "you don't want me to get the state police over here and shoot you. That's what it will come to if you don't calm down and give me that gun."

"I'm not going to give you this damned gun. I'm telling you to clear out." Suddenly he raised the shotgun and pointed it over the sheriff's head and pulled the trigger. There was a deafening blast as he fired into the air, beyond the porch. The deputy almost jumped out of his skin.

As soon as he saw Martinek raise the gun, the sheriff quickly stepped out of his line of sight by moving to the left of the door. He turned his body so his left shoulder was against the outside wall. He couldn't see Martinek except for his hands and the gun. It was a double-barrel shotgun, so the sheriff knew Martinek had one more shot left. "Clyde, that won't do. Just come out quietly, and we can talk peacefully."

Clyde raised the gun again. The sheriff could see it was pointed toward the sky. He pulled the trigger a second time; there was another ear-deafening blast, and some of the buckshot hit the ceiling of the porch, splintering the wood.

The sheriff knew he would have to act fast. Martinek didn't have another shell in his gun, but if he didn't move now, he would have time to reload. He rushed to the door with his pistol in his hand and slammed it down on Martinek's hand. That forced him to drop the gun. He stood facing Martinek with his pistol pointed at his chest. He shouted over his shoulder to his deputy. "Walt, get the hell in here!" The deputy started to run to the house, his gun in his hand. Speaking as calmly as he could muster, Kretzler said, "Now listen, Clyde. Calm down. Your gun's empty, and I'm not going to let you reload it. Just walk away from the gun and get down on the floor."

Martinek yielded. He was so drunk he couldn't even drop to the floor easily; he just fell down on his side. The sheriff shoved him with his foot so that he turned over on his belly. He told the deputy to handcuff him. Once he was secured, they helped him get up on his feet; they guided him out of the house, down the front steps, toward the police car.

They put him in the back of the police car, and the Deputy sat sideways in the front seat with his gun in his hand. He was clearly shaking.

"Sheriff, how did you do that? He had me scared to death, I could never do that."

"Not bad for a seventy-year-old, eh? They all think I'm decrepit and should retire. Maybe they'll think again."

They rode silently back to the jail in the Vinton courthouse. Martinek was passed out for the entire trip.

As soon as he got back to Vinton, the sheriff told his deputy to call WMT; he wanted the public to know that he had captured the murder suspect in the Truesdale killing in custody. Mosley did as he was asked.

Within minutes, an announcer on WMT Radio broke into the regularly scheduled program:

"We interrupt this program to announce that Sheriff Ralph Kretzler from Benton County has arrested a suspect in the murder of John Truesdale. The suspect is Clyde Martinek, a farmer living near Belle Plaine. The sheriff said he had resisted arrest and shot at him twice. He will be officially arraigned this afternoon or tomorrow. We will broadcast additional information on the five o'clock news."

That afternoon, a reporter from the *Cedar Rapids Gazette* even drove out to interview the sheriff.

"Do you think he killed Truesdale, Sheriff?" the reporter had asked. "That's what people are saying. How about the second guy, Caldwell?"

"We'll just have to wait and see. Martinek will have a hearing before the district judge, and we'll see what he has to say for himself. At a minimum, he'll spend some time in jail for resisting arrest, assaulting a police officer, and intoxication." The sheriff gave the reporter details about how he had captured Martinek. The reporter turned it into a juicy story that flattered the sheriff. The voters would be pleased.

Later that day, the sheriff briefed the prosecuting attorney. They went together to try to get Martinek to talk. All he kept saying was, "The dirty bastard got what he deserved; the dirty bastard got what he deserved. That's all I'll say."

By four in the afternoon, the prosecuting attorney was prepared to file an indictment against Martinek for the murder of Truesdale. He was not charged in the case of the second murder; it would take more time and investigation to decide to try him for that murder.

When Martinek told the judge he did not have enough money for a lawyer, the judge asked Harold Samuelson, Roy's good friend, to represent Martinek pro bono.

Samuelson was a good defense lawyer. He was sympathetic to the situation that defendants found themselves in, and he talked with them in a friendly way. They usually trusted him. He had trouble with Martinek because he wouldn't talk to him. As a result, when Martinek was brought before the district court judge, he automatically pled him not guilty. The judge had him bound over for trial. No date was set.

Chapter Eleven

Thursday, September 4, 1952

The starting point for the discussion at the next Rounders' meeting was Clyde Martinek's arrest and the news that the second body at Truesdale's farm belonged to his uncle.

Everyone was present including Sam Winfield. He knew the farmers at the end of his route would not be happy to get their mail late, but he wanted to know more about the arrest of Martinek. He found the Rounders' conversations informative; they seemed to have information from Vinton that no one else had.

Mac began. "Pansy, you were the one who told the sheriff about Martinek, weren't you?"

"Yes, he came in to get his truck worked on. He was pretty nasty. He said that his daughter was pregnant, and Truesdale was the father. He also said Truesdale got what he deserved."

"I told the sheriff the same things," Stoner said angrily. "But he didn't listen to me, the chauvinist pig."

"Maybe, but sheriff really put his neck on the line when he arrested him," Fritz said.

Mac asked, "Did Martinek actually shoot at the sheriff?"

"Not exactly," Fritz said. "I talked with his deputy; he said

Martinek shot over the sheriff's head. It was more as a warning. He was pretty brave. I think his deputy almost messed his pants."

"Poor guy," Stoner said; "I probably would have. Has the sheriff finally figured out that Martinek did it—like I said last time?"

"He's the sheriff's best candidate at this point," Fritz said.

Winfield spoke up. "He certainly had the motive and the opportunity, and we know he went over there to argue with him. Like you said last week, Fritz, Martinek must have killed the uncle because he saw him kill Truesdale".

"Well, that isn't exactly what I said, but I agree the uncle probably was murdered because he saw Truesdale killed."

"Does anybody know if he has confessed?" Mac asked.

"No, he hasn't," Fritz replied. "Walt said he wouldn't say one way or the other. He won't deny it, but he won't say he was guilty."

Lawrs said, "There are still loose ends that don't make sense. The uncle's pickup hasn't been discovered, and two different guns were used."

"Maybe he killed Truesdale with the shotgun, discovered the uncle had seen him, and used the handgun because it was more convenient—especially if the uncle was running to the chicken coop," Winfield offered.

"Makes sense to me," Stoner said.

Mac asked, "Can we assume now that there isn't any relationship between the murders at Truesdale's and the break in at Dot's?"

"I would think so," Fritz said. "Except for the dark trucks involved, there's not much to connect the two cases. It's hard to imagine that the uncle robs Dot, goes home, gets in a fight with Truesdale, and kills him. And if that's what happened, who killed the uncle?"

"Let's get back to Martinek," Roy said. "Is he the kind of guy who'd murder someone?"

"He sure is," Winfield said. "He can be nasty."

"I agree," Pansy said. "The day I saw him, he was swearing and really carrying on. Of course, he'd been drinking. He went to Kelley's while I was fixing his truck, and he came back pretty sloshed."

Fritz said, "He was drunk when the sheriff picked him up, so he probably was drunk when he argued with Truesdale."

"I agree," Winfield said.

"We're certainly not going to settle this here," Roy said in his usual, cautious manner. "Lawrs, you met Truesdale's cousins from Ohio, didn't you? What were they like?"

"They seemed liked good folks. They appreciated the fact that people were willing to help pick the corn. I also told them that I'd be interested in buying the place."

"Why would you do that?" Roy asked.

"I've been thinking about buying more land," Lawrs said. "If I had more, I could get a renter to crop-share; that way I could feed more cattle."

"But more land would mean more work, wouldn't it? You'd just have to hire someone to help, and you'd wind up not making any more than before," Roy suggested.

"Not so. On a bigger scale, you can afford more efficient equipment, and you can make more money."

"Goodness," Mac said. "I can remember when just having a horse and plow was enough. What they don't teach you in college. Next thing you'll be telling us is that the tractors operate themselves."

Stoner interjected "You don't want to get too busy, young man, or you'll not have time for the ladies." Then she added, "Sometime I think, Lawrs, you're a walking advertisement for that man Kinsey's book."

"Oh," Pansy said. "Lawrs was the one Kinsey interviewed." Everyone, including Lawrs, laughed.

"Thanks for the comic relief," Mac said. "Who knows how this will all work out in the end?"

"You're right," Lawrs said. "It reminds me of the predicament that Homer got himself in."

"Oh, no, Lawrs," Mac said. "You're too early. It's not time for everyone to go home."

"Well, Pansy looks like he's getting antsy, so I thought a joke would calm him down," Lawrs said.

"Well we might as well get the inevitable over with, Lawrs. Go ahead," Mac said.

Lawrs started. "Well, my friend Homer sued the railroad because a train had run over his prized bull. It carried him off on the front cowcatcher. He hadn't been seen since. Before the trial started, the big city lawyer for the railroad cornered Homer and tried to get him to settle the case for less than he was asking. Eventually, Homer agreed and took half of what he wanted. After Homer had the check, the lawyer gloated, 'I hate to tell you, old man, but I put one over on you. I probably couldn't have won; the engineer was asleep when he hit your bull.' 'Well, young feller,' Homer said, 'I was a bit worried about winning, too. The darned bull came home this morning.'"

Everyone laughed, and they switched the topic to talk about politics, a topic that came up at almost every Rounders' meeting. Stoner, Fritz, and Lawrs were Republicans. Roy, Mac, and Pansy were Democrats. Their arguments could get heated at times, but they all respected each other's opinions.

During July, the topic had been the conventions. Mac and Pansy had supported Kefauver, while Roy favored Stevenson. Fritz and Lawrs favored Eisenhower, while Stoner had supported Taft. No matter who wins, Stoner had said at the time, "Betty Furness is the real winner. I swear she was on TV more than anybody else. She's going to make a fortune for Westinghouse."

Most thought Eisenhower was probably a better choice than Taft. "He's the more likely of the two to bring this Korean War to an end," Pansy had said.

"You mean Korean Peace Action," Roy had corrected him. "Truman had to call it that because congress didn't declare war."

"He never asked them to declare war!" Stoner had said sharply.

Pansy had retorted, "Whatever you call it, we've got to get out of there. If we're not careful, we'll wind up in a full-scale war with China. Eisenhower's a better bet to shut it down than Taft is."

Today, with the campaigns in full swing and the elections only two months away, Pansy asked the group, "Did you heard about the mess Nixon got himself in? He's got a secret slush fund. Eisenhower's gonna have to dump him."

"Nonsense," Stoner replied. "I'm no fan of Nixon, but all those politicians have slush funds. He's no different than the rest."

"Oh, come on," Pansy countered. "Democrats don't have slush funds, just Republicans."

"We'd better change the subject," Mac said, always the peacemaker.

"Well, I've got to leave anyway," Pansy said. "I promised a guy I'd have his truck done by two."

Stoner said, "I've got to go, too, Mac. Thanks for the coffee; we don't tell you that often enough.

"You're welcome." Mac responded, good-naturedly, "It only costs me sixty cents a pound; when it gets to seventy-five I'll start charging."

Within a few minutes, everyone was gone except for Mac and Lawrs; he was staying for lunch—much to Ruthie's usual delight.

When Lawrs got to the counter, Ruthie put her plan into action. "Lawrs, like I said last week, you were really brave finding that man's body. You ought to run for sheriff."

"That would be too much for me," he said. "I wouldn't want to deal with murders all the time, but thanks Ruthie; I appreciate your compliment." He smiled at her.

She was pleased. She decided she would find other ways to pay him compliments. She would love to tell that him he was good-looking, but she wasn't sure this was the right time; maybe that would be too obvious.

"What will you have to eat, Lawrs?" she said as sweetly as she could.

"Just the regular," he said, "One of your Maid-Rites."

"You know we can't call them Maid-Rites, Lawrs," Ruthie said apologetically. "Mac says that it wouldn't be legal because she won't pay the fee to use that word."

"Okay, then, a loose meat sandwich and a Nehi." He paused. "You know what, I'll have a root beer today. What have you got? Hires?"

"No, Mason's," Ruthie replied. She was sorry she couldn't give him what he wanted.

"I'm striking out on all counts," Lawrs responded. "A Mason's it is." He reached over to pick up the morning *Des Moines Register*, which Mac had on the counter for people to read. He didn't look up until Ruthie brought him his sandwich. "Thanks," he said, and went back to reading.

Ruthie decided she shouldn't have told him that he couldn't call the sandwich a Maid-Rite. He must have taken offense; maybe he thought she was scolding him.

Lawrs finished his lunch, put down some money on the counter to cover the cost and a tip. As he left, he said simply, "See you next time, Ruthie."

She was upset; her plan hadn't worked. She'd have to think up something better the next time he stayed for lunch.

Chapter Twelve

Thursday Afternoon, September 4, 1952

Mac didn't think more about the murders after the Rounders left that morning. A young couple came into the cafe shortly after lunch and looked around the cases that held her Native American artifacts.

They seemed genuinely interested in them. They asked Mac what things were and how much they were worth. They also asked what tribe they came from. Mac liked them, and she spent more time than she usually did talking about the artifacts.

They were on their way to the state university in Iowa City. He was a graduate student, and they both came from Wyoming. Mac had a soft spot in her heart for Wyoming because that is where her son was killed; it was also where her first husband was buried. She didn't mention that to the young couple, but she did tell them that she was one-quarter Meskawaki, something she seldom told anybody.

The couple found Mac engaging and the artifacts impressed them. They stayed for a late lunch. When it came time for them to pay, Mac told them to put their money away; it was her treat. They protested, but as students, they didn't protest too much.

After they had gone, Mac thought how enjoyable they had been. It was a thought she carried with her most of the rest of the afternoon.

THE EVENING WAS HOT. IT had cooled off the past few days, but the August heat seemed to have returned, even though it was September. She had the air conditioner in the cafe going at high speed.

Business was slow, so she closed about eight-thirty. She turned off the lights and went back to her house.

It sat a few dozen yards behind the cabins she rented to tourists. She liked it back there because it allowed her to disconnect from the business of Midway. There were a couple of large elm trees on either side of the house. They shaded it most of the day, so it was relatively cool. She didn't have air conditioning in the house; she just used a fan.

Even though the house had been built around the turn of the century and needed some work, it was comfortable; pictures of her son and her first husband surrounded her. She also kept the best of her artifacts there, locked in a trunk. There was little to suggest that her second husband, Tom, lived there, too—at least when he wasn't driving his truck coast to coast.

Her usual routine before she went to bed was to watch television. She always tried to close a little before nine o'clock, so she didn't miss the beginning of any of her favorite shows, most of which started at nine. She especially liked *Texaco Star Theater* and the *Philco Television Playhouse.* On Sundays, she always watched the Ed Sullivan show. During the day, she listened to the radio. She had gotten hooked on a couple of the soap operas that Ruthie liked: *Guiding Light* and *Stella Dallas*—although she identified with Stella, whereas Ruthie identified with her daughter, Laurel, who had, as the announcer always said, 'married into wealth and society.'

TONIGHT THE NINE O'CLOCK SHOW was *Gangbusters*. After the show was over, she stayed up for the fifteen-minute news on WMT. At ten-fifteen, after the news was over, she went to bed.

She had trouble going to sleep this particular night. She tossed and turned, and then, just before she fell asleep, something caused her to look out her bedroom window. It looked east, and she could see the highway from Cedar Rapids.

She usually paid no attention to the traffic, but tonight she noticed a vehicle slowing down. It was cloudy, and there was no moonlight; she couldn't tell whether it was a car or a pickup. Through her open window, she heard it as it left the highway and pulled onto the gravel in front of the cafe where the gas pumps were. She couldn't see the front of the cafe from her house.

The first thing she thought was that they were going to try to steal gas. But she always turned the pumps off at night; she always did.

After a few minutes, when she didn't hear the car pull away through the gravel, she became concerned and decided to check.

She didn't put a light on, but she easily found her bathrobe and put on an old pair of shoes. Slippers would have been uncomfortable because she had to walk across the gravel between the cabins and the cafe. Tonight, none of the cabins were rented, so she wasn't concerned about being seen in her bathrobe.

As she left the house and passed between the middle two cabins, she saw a light in the cafe. It was moving. She was certain it was a flashlight. She kept the Hamm's beer neon sign over the bar on all night; so, in addition to seeing the moving light, she could see a silhouette of someone moving around inside.

She knew she had carried the cash register drawer back to the house. It was an automatic part of her routine, so she was certain the robber wouldn't get any money. But she did begin to worry about her artifacts.

Suddenly she remembered the young couple that had been there that afternoon. She wondered if their interest in the artifacts had motivated them to come back to steal them. Surely not. She was usually right in her judgment of people, and she hadn't judged them to be the type of people who would do such a thing.

Mac was not about to confront the burglar. She turned around and went back to her house. She wanted to call the sheriff, but since the phone in her house and the one in the cafe were on the same party line, she would have to ring for the operator, and the ring would be heard on the cafe's phone. She was concerned it would alert the burglar, and he would listen in.

After a moment or two, she thought that wouldn't necessarily be a bad thing. If the burglar heard her call the sheriff, he surely would get out of there quickly. On the other hand, if the burglar knew it would take twenty minutes for the sheriff to get there from Vinton, he would have more than enough time to steal what he wanted and get away safely.

Maybe, she thought, if he knew she lived behind the cabins, he might be brazen enough to come back there and try to steal some of her most highly prized artifacts, the ones she kept locked in a trunk in her house. If he did come to the house, he might kill her as someone had killed Truesdale.

Then it occurred to her that it was the same burglar that had broken into Dot's antique store. He would steal just her silver, just as he had done at Dot's.

As her mind was playing out all the possibilities, she remembered she hadn't told the young couple that she had her best artifacts in her house. If they were responsible for the break-in, they would have no reason to come back to her house. So far as she remembered, she hadn't even told them that she lived in a house behind the cabins.

She would call the sheriff.

She went to the telephone, picked up the receiver, and cranked the handle for a long ring. Mac knew it would take a few mintues for the operator to answer. The switchboard was in her living room, and if she were already in bed, she would have to get up to answer it.

After a few moments, she rang again. "This is the operator. How can I help you?" She sounded a bit grouchy, and her voice suggested that she had been asleep.

"Margaret, it's Mac at Midway. I'm being robbed. Call the sheriff."

The operator was suddenly alert. "I'll get Vinton, Mac."

There was an operator on the Vinton switchboard all night, so she answered right away. Mac explained the emergency, and the Vinton operator connected her with the sheriff's home.

Mac waited for what seemed like forever. When he answered, he said, "Mac, the night operator says you're having a break-in?"

"Yes, I saw his flashlight."

"He'll probably be gone before I can get there, but I'll come right away. Are you safe? For heaven's sake, don't confront him; you have no idea what he might do. Can you see his car?"

"No. He's out front by the pumps. I can't see out there from my house."

"I'm on my way. I won't use my siren, so maybe I can catch him. If he's gone when I get there, I'll honk; that way you will know it is safe to come out."

Just before Mac hung up, Margaret, the operator said, "Good Luck, Mac."

If waiting for the sheriff to come to the phone seemed a long time, the next twenty minutes were the longest of her life. She went back into her bedroom. She sat on the bed in the dark, listening.

At one point, she heard tires dig up the gravel as a car sped away. It didn't go back east. She continued to sit on the bed. A few more cars passed, but they didn't pull in or stop.

Finally, she heard the honk of the sheriff's car horn. It was a wonderful sound.

As she left her house, she realized she was in her bathrobe and old shoes. It didn't make any difference; the sheriff would not care.

She went to the front of the cafe. The sheriff was already out of his car, pointing a flashlight at the front door.

"Thanks for coming Ralph," she shouted.

"Are you okay?" He focused his flashlight on the ground in front of her, so she could walk toward him safely. As she got to the top step, the sheriff said, "He used a screwdriver or something to pry it open. You'll need a new lock." He added, "Let me go in first, just for safety's sake."

The screen door slapped behind him as he entered. He found the light switches quickly. He didn't turn the outside lights on, however, so it seemed strange to Mac to be standing outside in the dark, looking into the cafe through the front, lighted windows. She couldn't remember ever seeing it from this perspective.

The sheriff came back, holding the screen open for Mac. "He's long since gone."

Mac entered. She expected to find the large glass cases where her artifacts were kept smashed and empty. They were. The robber had taken everything!

She was distraught. It had taken years to assemble her collection. She knew it couldn't be duplicated. She felt violated.

Looking around, nothing else seemed to be missing.

"Are the Indian things the only things he got?" the sheriff asked.

She walked to where she kept some of her antiques on shelves and tables. At first, he could see nothing else missing. Then, she noticed that two boxes of sterling silver flatware were gone.

As she continued to look, she saw that the walnut box she had bought from Dot was also gone.

She called to the sheriff, who was standing on the other side of the room. “Some sterling flatware is missing, and a small box is gone, but it’s no loss.”

“What was in it?” the sheriff asked.

“A bible, an old county history, some old family pictures. Just junk. The box was worth more than what was in it. Ralph, I got it over at Dot’s after her break-in. Do you think there’s a connection to the break-in over there? They took silver both places.”

“The guy over there was driving a pickup; what was this guy driving?”

“I don’t know; I could only see his headlights.”

“I’ll go outside and see if I can find anything.” He turned on the outside lights and went out.

Mac drank a lot of coffee, and she knew the sheriff did, too. The pot behind the counter still had some coffee in it; she turned the hot plate on.

She went back to looking around. She didn’t see anything else missing.

The sheriff came back in and said, “Mac, I can’t see anything out there suspicious. I’ll come back tomorrow; maybe when it gets light, I can find some tire marks or something. Do you have an inventory of what’s missing? I don’t need it now; I can pick it up tomorrow.”

“I have an inventory in my house. I can get it tonight if you want.”

“That’s not necessary. Like I said, I’ll need to come back tomorrow when I can look outside better.”

“Okay. I will look around more carefully in the morning and see if anything else is missing. I’ve got my best artifacts back in my house, so at least he didn’t get them. Ralph, I thought you might like some coffee. Sorry, it’s just warmed up.”

“Absolutely.” Having been asleep when she called him, coffee would certainly hit the spot, fresh or warmed-up. Besides, in his long experience with situations like this, he knew that Mac would want to sit and talk with someone before he left. Talking about a crime sometimes took a little of the anxiety out of the situation for the victim.

She poured him a cup and one for herself. “Take anything in it?”

“No. Just black, no sugar.”

Suddenly she remembered the young couple. “Sheriff, I forgot. There was a young couple in here this afternoon; they were really interested in the artifacts. I spent a lot of time with them. They wanted to know where things were from and what they were worth. I thought they were real nice, but maybe they did it. I haven’t had anybody in here for a long time as interested in the artifacts.”

“Do you remember their names or where they were from?” the sheriff asked.

“He was Jack Blackstone. I remember because the beads on an item he looked at were black, and I thought it was a funny coincidence. Black beads aren’t common on the things I had.” She paused, “I don’t remember her name, but they were students—at least he is. They go to the university in Iowa City.”

“Well, it shouldn’t be hard to find them. After I swing by in the morning, I’ll go on down there and check with the sheriff in Johnson County.”

As he left, he said, “Shove something across the door for tonight. You’ll have to get someone to fix it tomorrow. How hard will the glass cases be to fix?”

“It’s beveled plate glass,” she said. “I’ll have to have it custom cut. It’ll take a week or so. There’s a place in Cedar Rapids that does it; I had them repair one of the cases a couple of years ago.”

After the sheriff had left, Mac pushed an antique bureau in front of the door. It wouldn’t keep someone out who was determined to get in, but at this point, she wasn’t going to worry about it. She decided she also wouldn't try to clean up the broken glass. She'd wait until morning. It was too depressing to look at the empty cases.

She went back to her house. Suddenly she was overcome with grief. It was almost as bad as when she'd found out that Todd was dead. Something else she loved had been taken from her life again. She cried quietly. Tom was in his truck on a run to the West Coast. She wished he were there. Maybe he would call tomorrow.

Chapter Thirteen

Friday, September 5, 1952

Sheriff Kretzler drove back to Midway about nine-thirty the next morning.

When he arrived, he looked around the outside of the cafe; he was searching for any clue to identify the previous night's robber. Mac had said she had heard a car kicking up gravel when it left, but he could not find anything helpful.

The sheriff went in to see Mac. Ruthie had just come in and was behind the counter; she was looking a bit helpless and disoriented. Mac was seated at the round table on the opposite side of the room. She had a small pile of papers in front of her.

"Hi, Mac. Did you find your inventory?"

"Yes, Ralph, I've been up since five. I wrote out a copy for you and cleaned up the mess."

"What do you figure they got?"

"Twenty-three artifacts and three sterling silver flatware sets. There's nothing else except for the small box, but I'm not going to worry about that."

The sheriff looked over at Ruthie behind the counter and mimed drinking a cup of coffee. She understood, poured a cup, and brought it to him.

"Did you have insurance, Mac?"

"Fortunately, some. I had a policy on the artifacts. They were covered for a thousand."

"Wow! I had no idea they were worth that much."

"They didn't get everything. I keep the best stuff in my house. What they got was worth about seven hundred plus the silver. I'll have to take a loss on it."

"It should be easy to trace the Indian things if someone tries to sell them," the sheriff said.

"If they know what they're doing," she responded, "they won't sell them around here. They'll drive to someplace like Santa Fe and sell them there."

"Should I send the inventory to the Santa Fe police?" Sheriff Kretzler asked.

"That would be great, Ralph. As long as you're at it, you might send one to the police in Albuquerque."

"I'll have my secretary type some carbon copies and send them to New Mexico the first of next week."

"Thanks, Ralph."

The sheriff continued to talk and drink his coffee. He thought Mac seemed a lot calmer this morning. He could tell last night that she was upset.

When he got ready to leave, he said, "Mac, I'll go down to Iowa City now, and see if I can find the couple you told me about last night. If they're students, the university will be able to track 'em down. You said his name was Blackstone, right?"

"Yes, Jack, if I remember correctly. I can't remember her name."

THE SHERIFF HAD BEEN TO Iowa City many times, and he knew the county courthouse was located just south of the central part of the university. To get there, he drove past the Old Capitol. Iowa City had been the capital of Iowa until it was moved to Des Moines in 1857. It was a graceful old limestone building with a gold dome. It sat in the middle of what was called the Quadrangle because there were four, nearly identical, old buildings on the four corners of the grounds.

He parked his car at the courthouse. It was a Romanesque structure, much larger than the one in Vinton. There was a tower in the center of the building; it extended three or four floors higher than the three-story heighth of the rest of the building.

When he went into sheriff's office, he identified himself to the secretary. He told her that he needed to speak to the sheriff on a criminal matter. He had his uniform on, and the secretary recognized his name.

She got up, knocked on the sheriff's door, opened it, and announced Sheriff Kretzler.

The sheriff of Johnson County was Jacob Phillips, a well-built man in his early-forties.

"Come in Ralph, haven't seen you for awhile. How can I help you? This is quite an honor—you coming down here yourself. It must be serious."

Kretzler told Phillips what had happened at Midway the previous night. He explained that a few hours before the robbery, two students from the university had come in, and they had been quite interested in Mac's Indian collection. "I'm not accusing them, you understand, but I'd like to talk with them to see if they know anything useful."

"Oh, I understand completely."

"Can you tell me how I can locate the man? His name is Jack Blackstone. I don't know his wife's name."

Sheriff Phillips told Kretzler that if he were enrolled, the university's registrar would know where he lived. He looked up the number and called the registrar's office. He identified himself to the woman who answered the phone and asked her to determine if she had a student named Jack Blackstone enrolled.

A few minutes later, after she had gone through the card files where students' names and addresses were kept, the woman gave him the address of a graduate student named Jack Blackstone; he was from Wyoming. His wife was also a student; her name was Elizabeth.

After he had hung up the phone, Phillips went over to the city map. "You're in luck. He's only about five blocks from here, on South Linn." He pointed to a location on the map. "There's a small apartment building there. Do you want me or my deputy to come along?"

"That would be appreciated. I have no idea what I'll find. It would be good to have someone from Johnson County there—just in case. I don't want to bother you; just send one of your deputies with me."

"Sure, glad to do it." Phillips took Kretzler to one of the deputies' offices and introduced him. He asked him to take Kretzler to the address he had received from the registrar. He explained that Kretzler would fill him in on whom he is looking for and why. He instructed the deputy to take one of the Johnson County sheriff's cars.

After thanking Phillips and promising to let him know what he discovered, Kretzler accompanied the deputy to the parking lot along the side of the courthouse. The deputy was closer to Kretzler's age than Phillips was, probably in his early sixties. He had lived in Iowa City all his life and knew the town well.

"The place we are going to was once an old potato chip factory, but you'll have a hard time believing that," he said. "A custodian at the university bought it a few years ago and really fixed it up. He added a second story. There are about six apartments."

As the sheriff had said, it was a short trip. They pulled into a small gravel parking lot and got out of the car. "He's in number three over there." He led the way down a short sidewalk at the back of the building. He knocked; a young woman answered the door.

"Elizabeth Blackstone?"

"Yes, can I help you?" She was obviously startled to see two men in uniforms at her door.

He introduced himself and Sheriff Kretzler. "Could we come in and talk with you?"

"Of course. Come in. I was just preparing lunch." Looking at a clock, she continued, "Jack should be home soon. His class let out ten minutes ago; it only takes a few minutes to walk here from East Hall."

Kretzler looked around. It was an unusual apartment. It was just one large room with high ceilings and large casement windows on two sides. The building was constructed of cinder block, which recently had been painted a pale, pastel green.

The only door to the apartment entered directly into a narrow Pullman kitchen. As you walked in, eight-foot high plywood walls separated a large corner of the room from the kitchen and the living area; the bedroom was behind the walls. The walls didn't go all the way to the top of the tall ceiling. Elizabeth walked a few steps into the area that served as a living room. There was a propane gas heater in one corner.

"Please sit down," she said. "I'm sure my Jack will be along soon." She took a swift breath and then exclaimed, "It's not about him; nothing's happened to him has it?"

"No, I'm sure your husband is perfectly fine. We just want to talk to you about your visit to the Midway cafe. I believe you were there yesterday?" Kretzler asked.

"Oh, yes, we were. Has something happened to it?"

Kretzler started to tell her about the robbery when the screen door in the kitchen opened; it wasn't visible from where they were standing in the living room. A man called out, "Liz, what's a sheriff's car doing out here?" The man walked into the living room area and stopped when he saw the two officers. "What's wrong? Is it something about my folks in Wyoming?"

"Honey, they're here about that place we stopped at yesterday; you know, the one with Native American artifacts and the nice lady, Mac."

The deputy introduced himself and Kretzler. "Ralph, why don't you take it from here?"

Jack asked them if they would like to sit down and pointed at two small chairs. The two officers sat down, and Jack and Elizabeth sat on a small couch across from them. That was all the furniture there was in the living room area except for a coffee table, a relatively large bookcase filled with academic-looking books, and a small TV.

Kretzler explained: "Last night Midway was robbed, and all of the owner's Indian artifacts were stolen. We know you were there yesterday, and we wondered if you could tell us anything that would help us catch the thief."

"Mac's things were stolen?" Elizabeth said. "Oh, that's terrible. She was so proud of them, and she seemed like such a nice lady. Was she hurt?"

"No, I'm glad to say she wasn't."

Jack looked intently at the two officers. "You don't think we had anything to do with it, do you? We just wouldn't do anything like that. You have to take my word for it."

"We're not accusing you of anything. We're just trying to run down any leads that could help us solve the case," Kretzler said. "Did you notice anything suspicious when you were there or as you were driving away?"

"No, I don't remember seeing anything unusual. Do you, Liz?"

"No, I don't." she said. "Were all of her things taken? Did they take more than the artifacts?"

"Several sets of sterling flatware are missing. Would you mind if I asked you where you were last evening? When did you get home?"

"Let me think," Jack said, looking at Elizabeth. "We were there about two in the afternoon. We probably spent forty-five minutes looking at the artifacts. Mac was so generous to tell us about them. I'm studying cultural anthropology, so everything was of great interest to me. We had a sandwich and left. I'd say that was somewhere around three-thirty or four. We drove straight on to Cedar Rapids and took highway 218 south to Iowa City. We got here just before six." He looked at his wife for confirmation.

She nodded her head and said, "That's about right."

He went on, "After we got in, we went upstairs to our neighbors. They're good friends. They live just above us. We went to dinner together. A place east of Cedar Rapids called the Lighthouse. They have dances, and we stayed 'til about eleven-thirty, wouldn't you say, Liz? We got home a little after midnight."

"You wouldn't mind if we asked your friends to confirm that, would you?" Kretzler asked.

"No, of course not," Jack answered. "Do you know if they're upstairs now, Liz?"

"I think so. I saw Nancy just a while ago. She was hanging some clothes on the line. I think I heard Dan on the steps a few minutes before these two officers knocked. I'll see if their car is here." She got up and walked back around to where the door was.

"Yes, their car is here," she said, even before reappearing around the wall partition. "I'll go up and get them. I'm sure they would be more than willing to come down. They're very nice. They're from Iowa." She added almost unconsciously, "Everyone from Iowa is nice."

"No, that won't be necessary," Kretzler said. "We'll just go up and explain ourselves. We don't need to bother you any more."

As they all rose from their seats, the deputy said, "This is a really nice place. I've driven by it, but I've never been inside. It's an unusual arrangement. It was an old potato chip factory wasn't it?"

Elizabeth responded, "Yes, it was. They gutted the place and created three apartments downstairs. They built a second story with three more. They're nicer than this one, but not as interesting, I guess. Ours just has this room besides the Pullman kitchen you entered through; the bedroom's behind that partition." She pointed to the open space that served as the entrance to the bedroom; there was no door. "Come look if you'd like. Please excuse the mess; I haven't had time to unpack everything."

Deputy Kramer walked over to the opening and looked around the corner. There was just a bed and one dresser. There wasn't even any closet, just a shelf with a rod underneath to hold clothes on hangers. There were boxes and suitcases on the floor.

"We were just lucky to get this place," Jack said. "Off-campus housing is hard to get—especially clean places like this. The owner keeps it real nice. He painted it when we were back in Wyoming on vacation; that's where we're from. He plants flowers and keeps the parking lot up. The snow is shoveled as soon as it comes down. There's even a separate laundry room with a free washer and dryer. It really is a find, compared to some of the other places."

The two officers expressed their appreciation for the time Jack and Elizabeth had given them. Jack accompanied them as they went out; he pointed to a set of wooden stairs that ran to the second floor. "It's just up there—number six. Their names are Nancy and Dan Winslow. They're students, too."

The two officers walked up the stairs. They knocked on number six. A young man came to the door. The deputy introduced himself and Sheriff Kretzler. He asked if they could come in.

Once they were inside, Kretzler explained that they were just trying to track down anyone who might know about the robbery; he described what was taken. He told them that they had just left the Blackstones' apartment, and that they had visited Midway only a few hours before it was robbed.

"I understand they had supper with you last night. Is that right?"

Dan answered that they had. The officers asked where they had gone, and when they had come back. Nancy explained they had gone to the Lighthouse and stayed there, dancing until about eleven-thirty. "We got home about twelve-thirty," she said.

They assured the officers that the students living downstairs were honest; they said they couldn't believe they might be involved in anything like a robbery. Appreciation was expressed, hands shaken, and goodbyes said.

Waiting until they were in the car, the deputy told Ralph that he had specifically accepted Elizabeth's invitation to look into the bedroom; he wanted to see if anything there might connect them to the robbery.

Kretzler told him that he knew that was why he had looked and asked, "I assume you didn't see anything suspicious, did you?"

"No, absolutely not." He described what he had seen.

They drove back to the courthouse where they reported to Sheriff Phillips. Kretzler told him that he was satisfied the young couple had nothing to do with the robbery, thanked him, and left.

On his way back to Vinton, Kretzler stopped at Midway and told Mac that it didn't appear as though Jack and Elizabeth Blackstone were involved.

"If there is a silver lining to this cloud," she said, "it's that my judgment of those young people wasn't wrong. They seemed so nice. You meet all kinds when you run a place like this, and they were some of the better ones."

Chapter Fourteen

Tuesday, September 9, 1952

Ruthie came in at nine-thirty as scheduled. She stayed past the supper hour, usually until about five-thirty or six, depending on how busy they were. Mac opened up and closed the place down.

Ruthie was excited as she put on her apron. “Mac, you’ll never believe it. I saw Audrey Martinek, Shelia’s mother, at the grocery store last night. I asked her about Shelia. I told her that I’d heard she was pregnant. She told me that it was true, but when I asked about the father, she said she didn’t think it was Truesdale.”

“What?” Mac asked with disbelief.

“Yes, that’s what she said. I was shocked, but it wasn’t the kind of place we could talk. Mac, I told her that you’d be glad to see her, and you’d buy her lunch if she came in. I hope that was okay. I figured you could get her to tell you what she knew.”

“Of course,” Mac said. “I’d like to know what she has to say.”

At eleven o’clock, Mac put on her apron and took over the counter; Ruthie always took a break before the lunch crowd arrived. Today, there were two men in the cafe having lunch. About ten minutes after they left, Audrey Martinek came in.

“Hi, Audrey. How are you?” Mac asked. “Haven’t seen you in a long spell. I'm glad Ruthie told you to drop in. I hope you'll let me buy you lunch."

"Oh, that would be so nice, thank you, Mac." She was a short woman and had to work hard to get up on the stool at the counter.

"I heard about Clyde getting arrested," Mac said.

"Yeah, it was a shock to both me and Ruthie." She seemed to want to tell Mac everything. "When I divorced him, I got nothing—just an old rental house. He sends me a little check every month, but it doesn't even cover the gas and lights. It needs fixing, but he won't pay for it. Now he'll have to pay that lawyer Samuelson, and I won't get anything." She paused and then continued, "He threw Shelia out when he found out she was pregnant. You know she's expecting don't you?"

"I'd heard."

"He called her names, and said he wouldn't give her no money."

Audrey continued, "I've only got one bed, but she's staying with me. She helps with the bills, but she's not going to be able to work much longer; the baby will be here in a few months."

Mac said, "I had heard you were going to take care of the baby, and she would go back to work as soon as it came."

"Yeah, that was the plan, but what with Clyde going and gettin' himself arrested, everything's up in the air. Maybe, if they find him guilty, Shelia can get the house he's living in, and we can sell mine. That would be worth something."

"Do you think Clyde killed Truesdale?" Mac asked.

"Don't know. He's a mean old cuss, and for sure he could've done it, but he told Shelia somebody else got to Truesdale first."

"Yes, I heard that, too," Mac said. She added, "What a mess for you. I'm so sorry for what you're going through."

Mac did feel sorry for Audrey. She was dressed poorly. She looked whipped. Mac didn't know her ex-husband well, but from what she did know, living with him would have been hell. It also explained a little about Shelia. She probably dated to escape her life at home. In another situation, both Audrey and Shelia might have been confident, friendly, and out-going, but their life with Martinek hadn't allowed either of them to blossom and become the women they could have been. Mac was lucky, her first husband had been loving and supportive; her current husband, Tom, was always respectful and attentive—even though he was gone much of the time.

"I heard that Shelia told her dad that Truesdale was the father of her baby. Is that true?"

"Yes, that's what she told 'em both. That's the reason Clyde's so mad. But I'm not so sure," she added. "I shouldn't say this about my daughter, Mac, but Truesdale wasn't the only person she went out with—if you get my drift."

"Then why would she tell Truesdale he was the father?"

"Honest? She thought she could get child support, or that he might marry her. But he was just as mad as her dad was, and he said he wouldn't help neither."

"Who is the dad?"

"She doesn't know." Audrey continued, "Now that Truesdale's dead, she's sticking to her story because she thinks she might get some of his estate."

"She shouldn't get her hopes up," Mac said. "I understand Truesdale didn't have any money. When they sell his place, it'll all go to pay off his debts. Besides, it would be almost impossible to convince a court that she was entitled to some of his estate."

"She doesn't know that," Shelia's mother said, somewhat startled.

"Have either of you talked to Clyde since he's been in jail?"

"He won't even see me—or her."

"That's too bad," Mac said. "Oh, I just feel so sorry for you."

At that point, two men came in for lunch, so Audrey and Mac stopped talking about Shelia and the murder. Mac wouldn't let

Audrey pay for her sandwich or drink. She even served her a piece of pie. Audrey thanked her and left.

As soon as the lunch period rush was over, Mac left Ruthie in charge and went back to her house. She phoned Stoner to tell her what Shelia's mother had said.

Stoner responded by saying, "Boy, if that doesn't beat all. She sure let on to me it was Truesdale, and she said it loud enough everybody in the place could hear."

Mac replied, "Well if he isn't the father, that really throws the theory that Clyde killed Truesdale into a cocked hat."

"No, it doesn't," Stoner said authoritatively. "As long as Old Man Martinek thought Truesdale was the father, he'd have a motivation for killing him." —She emphasized the word thought.

"I guess that's right," Mac replied tentatively. And then, with more certainty, she said, "You're absolutely right. Whether or not he's the father, it doesn't let him off the hook."

"Won't the Rounders be surprised when they hear all this?" Stoner said.

Mac went back to the cafe and sat at her round table. What a sordid world, she thought. Even with the tragedy she had experienced, it was infinitely better than Audrey's life. Could Shelia still make something of herself? She was on a downhill course that it would take more than luck to change. Mac wondered what would have become of her son, Todd, had he lived.

Chapter Fifteen

Wednesday, September 10, 1952

Roy had to go to Vinton again. Usually, he only went there every other month or so; twice in such a short period of time was unusual. However, a farmer from near Keystone had come to his house and asked him to find out who held the deed to a property he was interested in buying. Roy also planned to look up the boundary between Bill Robinson's property and Truesdale's farm.

He hoped he could have lunch with his friend, Everett Samuelson, who had accepted the job of defending Clyde Martinek. He was curious about what kind of defense he was going to use. It would be a busy day.

He had been unable to find anyone who would take him to Vinton, so he was left with his only other option—the bus. The bus stop was at the Herring Hotel. He got there several minutes before it was scheduled to leave at nine-fifteen, but it didn't arrive until ten-thirty. As a result, he didn't arrive in Vinton until eleven forty-five. The return bus left at three o'clock; he would have to work fast.

He planned to go to the courthouse first, but since the county clerk's office was closed from noon to one, he decided to start by talking with Samuelson. He thought he would have information about the two murders and the primary suspect, Martinek, that hadn't gotten into the gossip mill. He hoped that they could have lunch.

He was in luck. Everett was in his office, and he had no plans for lunch. They went to the cafe where they had eaten the last time Roy had been in Vinton.

After they had sat down, Roy asked his friend about his wife and children. Roy knew his wife and his two children. His son, his oldest child, had gone to Yale Law School and was practicing commercial law in New York City. Roy always gave Samuelson a hard time about the fact that he was a traitor to Harvard when he sent his son to Yale. His daughter had gone to college in Chicago and was a social worker there.

After the waitress had taken their order, Roy said, "Everett, you must have your hands full trying to figure out a defense for Martinek."

"Yes," he answered, "It's been hard to know how to defend him. He won't talk to me. He just keeps swearing and saying Truesdale got what was coming to him."

Samuelson continued. "But, there isn't any physical evidence that links him to the murder. There really isn't even any circumstantial evidence that points to him—except the story about his daughter and what he said to Frank O'Malley. No one can even identify him as the man who had an argument with Truesdale. If the sheriff doesn't release him, I'm going to file a *writ of habeas corpus* to have him released."

"But, he had a motive, and he said he wanted something bad to happen to Truesdale."

"I'd hate to lock everybody up who held a grudge against someone and secretly wanted him dead. There wouldn't be too many of us left."

"You're right, of course." Roy shifted the subject, "Was the shotgun he threatened the sheriff with the same one that killed Truesdale?" Roy asked.

"They can't be sure. If it had been a pistol or a rifle, they could have done a ballistics test, but you can't do that easily with a shotgun blast."

"Were there any fingerprints on the gun?" he asked. Then he answered his own question, "Of course not, the gun was Martinek's to begin with. Have they found any other guns?"

"No, there were no guns in Truesdale's house although there were some unused shotgun shells. There were no weapons at Martinek's except, of course, the shotgun he had with him when they arrested him."

"What about Truesdale's uncle? Do they think Martinek killed him, too?" Roy asked.

"Sheriff Kretzler has some doubts about that."

"Oh, really?"

"Yes, first of all, they think the uncle was shot before Truesdale died. The uncle's body was in much worse shape."

"But wasn't the fact that the chicken coop had to be hotter than the house a possible explanation for why that body deteriorated faster?"

Samuelson replied, "Possibly, but apparently there was so much difference in the state of the two bodies, they think the uncle died first. That makes it unlikely that Martinek killed the uncle—why would he shoot the uncle hours or days before he killed Truesdale?"

"If they think the uncle died first, doesn't that make it more likely that Truesdale could have killed him?"

"I suppose, but then, that doesn't explain who killed Truesdale."

"Unless it was Martinek."

"Maybe, but he's my client and I got to give him the benefit of the doubt."

"Does Martinek have an alibi?" Roy asked.

"As I said, he won't talk to me, and none of his neighbors know where he was about the time of the murder."

"What about his ex-wife or his daughter? Wouldn't they be more likely to know?

"As I understand it," Samuelson answered, "he and his wife were divorced, living apart, and I understand he had thrown his daughter out of his house—although he hasn't told me that, so I have to be careful about what conclusions I come to."

"Did you hear what he said to Pansy O'Malley? Pansy said he acted almost insane, and Mildred Stone says his daughter told her that her father had threatened Truesdale."

"Yes, I know about what happened at O'Malley's and what his daughter said to Stone," Samuelson said. "Actually, I'm not surprised. That's the way he is when I try to talk to him."

"I can really appreciate how difficult this must be for you. When do you think you might file a writ to get him out?" Roy asked.

"Well, I'm going to wait another couple of days. I could do it sooner, but I don't want to put the sheriff or the judge in a tight spot. If some concrete evidence doesn't emerge soon, however, they will have to let him go no matter whether they want to keep him in jail or not."

"Boy, that will upset the community." Roy said, "Everybody thinks he did it."

"I understand," Samuelson said. "But unless they can come up with more evidence than they have now, as far as I'm concerned, I've got to assume he's innocent."

"I was also wondering about a will for Truesdale. He didn't seem to have any money, but if a beneficiary in the will didn't know that, and he thought he had money, he might want him dead. Have they found one?" Roy asked.

"I don't think he had a will. I've asked around. No lawyer here in

Vinton prepared one, and the sheriff couldn't find one in his house. Kretzler even called around to banks to see if he had a safe deposit box where it might be kept. No luck."

They talked a bit longer—the usual stuff: the weather and politics. Roy thanked Samuelson for lunch and left. Samuelson went back to his office.

Roy looked at his watch; it was already one-fifteen. He would have to hurry. Fortunately, the courthouse was just across the street.

As he entered recorder's office, Jessie, the clerk, greeted him. Roy asked to inspect the property records again.

"You must be about to buy some land, Roy, what with all your interest in property records," Jessie said in jest.

"Not, me," Roy responded. "I've got a client who wants to buy a piece of land; he needs me to find the name of the current owner. Another client wants me to check the boundaries on his property; he owns the land behind Truesdale, the guy that got murdered. He wants to be sure what the boundaries are, so that if Truesdale's heirs sell the property, things don't get messy.

It took quite a while to find the name of the owner of the property near Keystone his client was looking for. The client had given him a rough, hand-drawn map of the area, but it didn't conform to the official plat maps. He finally figured it out by a process of elimination.

He had no trouble finding the legal description of Robinson's property. Fortunately, there was a line on the plat map indicating where the ravine was. It was as he had said: there was a small piece of land on Truesdale's side of the ravine that belonged to Robinson.

He checked the legal description for the Truesdale property. He wanted to see if an easement ran across his property to the small chuck of land that Robinson owned. An easement would make it easier for Robinson to access the land rather than building some kind of road or bridge across the ravine. There was no easement listed on the property description.

He would report what he found to both clients.

By the time he was finished, it was almost two-thirty. There wasn't time to go to the clerk of the court's office to withdraw the request to open Winfield's adoption records. If he missed the bus, he would have no way to get home. He was back in Belle Plaine by four-thirty.

Chapter Sixteen

Thursday, September 11, 1952

When Rounders met again, the glass cabinets where Mac kept her Meskawaki artifacts had not been repaired although everything had been cleaned up.

Everyone wanted to know about the break-in. Mac told the whole story with lots of details. She was obviously upset when she told them about losing her artifacts; she even choked up for a moment—something that was out of character with her usual, restrained demeanor. Everyone around the table knew what they meant to her.

To finish her story, Mac said that the only other things the burglar took were the sterling silver flatware sets and the small walnut box she had bought from Dot.

They asked her why she thought anyone would want the box. She had no explanation.

Mac told them about the young couple from the university. She said she felt guilty, thinking they might have stolen the artifacts—especially after the sheriff had gone to Iowa City and concluded they were not involved.

Stoner, no supporter of the sheriff, acknowledged he had at least followed through on the robbery at Mac's. "I guess he does some things right," she said grudgingly.

Then they processed the other big news: Mac's discussion with Shelia Martinek's mother, Audrey. Mac told them how Ruthie had run into her at the grocery store and invited her to come over to Midway for lunch. She told them that Shelia's mother wasn't sure that Truesdale was the father of Shelia's unborn child—even though she had told both her father and Truesdale that he was.

Mac explained that Shelia was naming Truesdale as the father in the hope she could get money out of him. Even after he died, she went on telling people he was the father, thinking that she might get money out of the estate. Mac reported that she had told Shelia's mother that after all his debts were settled, it would be unlikely there would be any money in the estate.

Lawrs suggested that if Truesdale were not the father, it would eliminate Martinek's motive for shooting him. Stoner quickly pointed out, as she had to Mac, that as long as Martinek thought Truesdale had impregnated his daughter, he could be the killer—even if his daughter's story weren't true.

It was juicy information, just as juicy as Lawrs finding the second body in the chicken coop, and the sheriff arresting Martinek.

Roy reported that Samuelson had said that the sheriff didn't have much of a case against Martinek, and he would probably have to let him go. He also told them what they already knew: that the uncle had been shot with a pistol and Truesdale with a shotgun. He said that Samuelson had told him that no guns were found on Truesdale's property, and the only gun Martinek had was the gun he used to threaten the sheriff. He said there was no way of proving Martinek's shotgun killed Truesdale. He also told the group that the sheriff thought the uncle had been killed before Truesdale had been killed because his body was in much worse condition.

They argued at length about who was killed first and why. If the uncle was killed first, who killed Truesdale? Why? It had to be Martinek. Roy remained skeptical. His colleagues assumed it was his general demeanor and legal training that kept him from drawing quick conclusions. The arguments went on until about eleven. At that point, Pansy was ready to go home, and he asked Lawrs if he had a joke.

Lawrs obliged: "Well, speaking of chicken coops, here's one about a city man who was tired of the urban rat race. He decided to give up city life, move to the country, and become a chicken farmer. He bought a nice chicken farm and moved in. His next-door neighbor was Homer—"

Pansy broke in and said with a laugh, "Boy, Homer sure gets around; go on."

"Well, one day Homer came over for a visit. He said to the city fellow, 'Chicken farming ain't easy. Tell you what: to help you get started, I'll give you a hundred chicks.' The city man was thrilled. Two weeks later Homer dropped by to see how things were going. The city fellow said, 'Not too well. All of the chickens you gave me died.' Homer said, 'I can't believe that; I've never had any trouble with my chickens. I'll give you a hundred more.' Another two weeks passed, and Homer stopped by again. The city fellow said, 'You're not going to believe this, but the other chickens died too.' Homer asked, 'For heaven's sake, what went wrong?' The city man said, 'Well, I'm not sure whether I'm planting them too deep or too close together.'"

It was a good joke and everyone laughed. Pansy commented on the fact that Lawrs frequently came up with jokes that were tied to what they were discussing.

With that, the meeting broke up. Just as they were leaving, Winfield came in with the mail. He was disappointed not to be have been able to sit in on the discussion.

When Lawrs went to the counter to have lunch, Roy came over and stood beside him. "I looked up the property lines between

Robinson and Truesdale," he said. "Robinson is correct. He owns land on the other side of the ravine, on Truesdale's side."

"That's good," Lawrs said. "When are you going to tell him?"

"I'll do it tomorrow."

Roy thanked Lawrs again for the referral; every little bit of money helped. He went out to the parking lot. Pansy was fuming again. Lately, it seemed to him that Roy was always slow getting out to his truck for the return trip to Belle Plaine.

After Roy had left, Ruthie deployed a new plan. "Hi, Lawrs, could you help me? I've got to bring a few cases of beer over here so I can put them in the cooler as we use them up."

Mac usually moved them each morning when she opened up the cafe, but this morning, Ruthie had specifically asked her not to do it; she explained that she was going to ask Lawrs to move them. Mac knew exactly why she wanted to ask him for help, so she went along with Ruthie's request. Besides, Mac said to herself, it would be nice to have someone else do it for a change.

Lawrs was his usual, friendly self when she asked for his help. "Sure, Ruthie. Just tell me where they are and where you want them."

"They're back here," she said, pointing to the door to the kitchen. "They're back on the porch."

As they moved through the kitchen to the closed-in porch, Ruthie pointed to the large grill. "If you ever want a steak for lunch, just let me know. We light the grill about eleven every morning, so it would be real easy to do one for you. How do you like them? I'll bet you go for rare."

"Good guess, Ruthie. You're right, but I prefer my steak at night; you know, in a nice restaurant or a dance place."

"Oh that sounds wonderful. Where do you go?"

"I like to go to the Lighthouse. It's on the other side of Cedar Rapids, just east of Mount Vernon. They've got great steaks, good music, and dancing."

"Do they do the Bunny Hop? I've always wanted to see it."

"Yeah, they just started doing it a month or so ago."

"That sounds so exciting." Now she made her big move. "I'd love to go over with you sometime, Lawrs."

"Sure, Ruthie, a bunch of us go together, usually on Saturday nights. I'll let you know when we go next time, and you can come with us."

"Thanks, Lawrs, that would be wonderful." She'd hit pay dirt.

"How many of these do you want?" Lawrs asked, standing over the stack of wooden beer cases."

"Three would be great."

"That won't be too hard."

"Oh, Lawrs, you shouldn't try to move them all at once. You'll strain yourself."

"When you're used to throwing around ninety-pound bales of hay, this is a snap."

"Oh, Lawrs, I've never seen anyone lift three at once. Be careful."

"It's okay," he said. He picked them up. They were very heavy. He decided he should have picked up just two, but he had already bragged to Ruthie about lifting three. He didn't want to lose face.

She replied, "I'll show you where they go."

Returning to the cafe, she went behind the bar and pointed to a place by the cooler where she wanted them. There was no one else in the cafe at the moment, so she shouted over to Mac, who was sitting at her table, "Mac, look, Lawrs moved three cases at one time."

"That's nice, Lawrs. Thanks. Ruthie and I usually have to move them ourselves, but we can only manage one at a time."

Ruthie seconded Mac, "Lawrs, thank you so much. I hope you didn't hurt yourself. Would you like a cool one? It's on me."

"No thanks, Ruthie. It has to be a special occasion to have one during the day."

If this isn't a special occasion, Ruthie thought to herself, I don't know what is. It was all working out much better than she hoped.

"What would you like to eat? The usual?" she asked.

"Yeah, I know I'm not suppose to call them Maid-Rites, but they're really good."

"Mac has a secret ingredient," Ruthie said. "After we steam the meat and rinse the grease off, she puts vinegar and lots of onion powder in it. She also dissolves bullion cubes in it. That's beside the salt and pepper, of course."

"Well, they're really good, whatever she does to them," Lawrs said.

The ground round was steamed and kept warm in a metal cooker underneath the counter, so Ruthie continued to face Lawrs as she prepared his sandwich. "I sure hope you didn't get your nice t-shirt dirty when you lifted those cases of beer. It's new isn't it?"

"Naw, I've had it awhile."

"It sure looks new. White looks good on you, especially with your tan," Ruthie said, trying to get something more going.

"Thanks, and that's a pretty blouse you're wearing, Ruthie. It goes with your eyes," he said.

Ruthie was in seventh heaven. This was working out better than she hoped.

"Oh, thank you Lawrs," she said as coyly as she could without being too gushy.

Unfortunately, at that moment, someone came into the cafe that Lawrs knew. "Hi, Harry. You going to the game in Ames next weekend?"

"Hi, Lawrs. I sure plan to. Are you going?"

They started to talk football and the prospects for Iowa State's team this year. Ruthie could have shot Harry for coming in just when she was making progress with Lawrs. She'd have to have another plan for next Thursday.

Chapter Seventeen

Friday, September 12, 1952

Lawrs asked himself where the gun was that had been used to kill Truesdale's uncle. He had discovered the uncle's body; maybe if he had looked more closely, he could find the gun.

After his morning chores on the farm were done, he got in his pickup and went back to Truesdale's farm. He got there about eleven o'clock. Truesdale's cousins from Ohio weren't there, and the house was locked.

He focused his attention on other places on the farm. Besides, he said to himself, the sheriff said he had searched the house carefully.

His first stop was the barn. He went down to the lower level where the steers were kept at night and during snowstorms; he looked through the feeding troughs, using a pitchfork he found there.

Next, he went around to the second level of the barn and did the same thing. To a certain extent, he thought, it was futile to search the barn; a handgun was so small, it could be anywhere.

He climbed up to the hayloft. It would be difficult finding anything up there, especially if the hay weren't bailed. It was bailed, so all that he could do was look around the stacks, if not within individual bales. He spent about fifteen minutes and found nothing.

He went on to the corncrib. Again, it would be difficult to find anything, either in the loose corn on the right side of the building or the oats on the other side. He still had the pitchfork with him, and he dug it into several places in both of the bins. Nothing.

He examined the middle part of the building, where the tractor and the wagon used to haul grain were kept. Seeing the age of the tractor and the somewhat decrepit look of the wagon, he was reminded of how broke Truesdale had been. He couldn't figure out what equipment he had bought from the implement dealer in Belle Plaine that would have caused a lien to be placed on the property. He also remembered that Truesdale didn't have a corn picker.

That thought triggered the idea that maybe someone had murdered Truesdale because he owed him money. Maybe he had other debts no one even knew about.

As he thought about it, however, he realized that if Truesdale owed money to someone, that person wouldn't want to kill the man who owed it to him. He'd never get the money then. Maybe he came to collect, they got into a fight, and the creditor accidentally killed him. Maybe the uncle came on the scene, discovered him killing Truesdale, and he had to be killed to keep him from talking.

Could it have been the other way around? Suppose Truesdale had bought a new tractor and other equipment, including a corn picker, from the dealer. Suppose he sold everything to someone privately to get cash. Maybe that person killed him in order not to have to pay him.

Stop it, Lawrs finally said to himself; he was just making up stuff that had little possibility of being true.

He then went to the small tool shed where there was a workbench, a variety of tools, and supplies such as barbed wire, nails, shovels, and rope.

He didn't stop at the chicken coop. He assumed the sheriff had examined it carefully; besides, it reminded him too much of what he had found there.

The only other place to look was the row of small, individual farrowing sheds out in back where sows were confined just before and after they gave birth. There were at least a dozen of them. The sheriff probably wouldn't have looked out there.

He walked to where they were located. One by one, he leaned over and looked inside, pushing the pitchfork around. All of them were empty.

When he had finished the last shed, he stood, trying to figure out where else he might look. He could see the row of scrub trees and brush that marked the edge of the ravine that Robinson believed was on his land. He didn't expect to find anything there, but he decided it was the only place he hadn't looked except the house and the chicken coop.

When he got to the edge of the ravine, he looked in both directions. His effort was rewarded. There, about two hundred feet to his left, was a dark blue Ford pickup. It was upright, at the bottom of the deepest part of the ravine where it couldn't be seen except by standing at the ravine's edge.

He walked along the edge of the ravine to where the truck was. He cautiously climbed down to it. He was sure it was a 1948 Ford, and it had black Ohio license plates. He was excited.

He stood beside the driver's front door. The window was down, and he could look inside. There, in plain sight, was a revolver on the passenger side of the seat.

Realizing it might have fingerprints on it, he didn't touch it. He climbed out of the ravine and stood, looking at the pickup. He knew from Roy that the truck was on Robinson's land. Maybe Robinson and Truesdale got into it again, and he killed him—on purpose or accidentally. The uncle could have seen what happened, and he had to be killed. Then, to hide what he'd done, at least until he could figure out a better way to dispose of the pickup, he drove it into the ravine. That solved the problem of a get-away car: he could just walk home.

Lawrs continued to speculate about what might have happened. Perhaps he was going to put the uncle's body into the truck, drive it someplace and leave it there. It might look like the uncle had shot Truesdale, driven off, and committed suicide. Maybe that is why he had left the gun in the front seat. Yes, that would explain everything.

His mind was still going a thousand miles an hour, but he knew he needed to tell the sheriff what he had found.

He went to Jim Ross' place across the road to phone the sheriff for the second time.

Jim was in the house, having lunch when he knocked. The inside door was open, and he could see through the screen.

Opening it, he said, "Jim, you won't believe it. I found the revolver that was probably used to kill Truesdale's uncle, and I found his truck. I need to call the sheriff again."

Jim jumped up from the table and came over to the door. "Come on." He led him to the phone in the dining room.

Jim's wife had gotten up at the same time her husband had, and she was standing beside him. "Where was it? How did you find it?" she asked.

"Give me a second," Lawrs said. "Let me ring the sheriff first." He rang the handle one long ring. Jane, the operator, answered almost immediately; he remembered her name.

"Jane, Lawrs Jensen at Jim Ross' house. I've found something the sheriff will want to know about immediately!"

"Not another body!" she exclaimed.

"No. A gun. Please get the sheriff."

As he waited for Jane to put the call through, he turned to Jim and Shirley. "I thought it was funny that the gun and the truck were still missing. I decided it was worth another look."

Impatiently, Jim asked, "Where were they?"

"In the ravine in back. There was the pickup, and the gun was in the front seat."

"The uncle's truck was in the ravine between Robinson's place and Truesdale's?" Jim asked.

"You mean the pickup truck the uncle was driving?" Shirley asked, as though she hadn't heard her husband's question.

Before he could answer, the sheriff was on the line. "What have you found this time, Lawrs?" Lawrs could tell from the tone of his voice Kretzler wasn't happy to hear from him again.

"Sheriff, I found the gun that was probably used to kill Truesdale's uncle. It's in the uncle's truck down in a ravine behind the farm. It's a blue forty-eight Ford pickup, just like Pansy said he was driving; it has Ohio license plates. The gun was in the front seat. I didn't touch it. I figured it might have finger prints."

"I'm going to have to hire you as my deputy," the sheriff said, cynically. "I'll be right over. It'll take twenty minutes. Stay there. In the meantime, don't you dare call WMT!"

He hung up before Lawrs could say anything.

"Maybe this will help the sheriff solve this thing," Jim said. "I assume he's coming right over?"

Lawrs responded. "He said twenty minutes. He said we shouldn't call WMT."

Jim's wife laughed. "By this time, if someone had been listening in on the party line, we'd have known." She paused. "Do you suppose Robinson could have killed him?" she asked, turning to her husband and looking worried.

"At this point," Jim said, "I don't know what to think."

"I agree with Shirley," Lawrs said. "The truck being in the ravine between the two places is suspicious. Maybe, Robinson and

Truesdale were arguing, not Martinek. That's why you wouldn't have seen him drive away."

"Good point," Jim said.

"But, why would he kill the uncle?" Shirley asked.

Jim hypothesized, "Maybe the uncle saw Robinson kill Truesdale, so Robinson and had to kill him and ditch the car in the ravine." He smiled, "no pun intended."

Lawrs agreed. "Yes, but the problem is that the sheriff thinks the uncle was killed first."

"Why do they think that?"

"Both bodies were in bad condition, but the uncle's was worse—or, so the sheriff says."

"Yes, but it had been out in the chicken coop where it was so much hotter." Jim said.

"Absolutely," Lawrs said. "I don't care whether it was in the house or in the chicken coop; it was damned hot both places. Remember, it was over a hundred degrees at the time."

He went on. "Seeing the gun in the truck made be think about why there were two different guns. Suppose Robinson wanted to make it look like the uncle had committed suicide after he shot Truesdale. Rather than use the shotgun he had killed Truesdale with, he used a revolver. The bullet in the uncle's head is where you might shoot yourself."

"I don't understand," Shirley said. "Why would the uncle have been in the chicken coop? Why wouldn't the body be in the truck?"

"I don't know," Lawrs said. "Maybe he panicked, left the uncle where he shot him, and drove the truck into the ravine until he figured out how to get the body away from the farm."

Shirley interrupted. "We're not going to solve it all right now. Lawrs, we were just having lunch. Egg salad sandwiches. I've got some I was saving for the kids' snack when they came back from school. Would you like some? I can always find them something else."

"That would be great," Lawrs said. "All that tromping around over there made me hungry."

They returned to the table. Jim and Lawrs sat down while Shirley fixed a sandwich. They discussed everything again. Lawrs explained where he had looked before finding the truck.

When the sheriff arrived, he didn't look happy, but he didn't say anything except that he wanted to see the truck and the gun—it was almost as if he didn't believe Lawrs.

Lawrs took the sheriff and his deputy, who had come with the sheriff, to the ravine. Jim went with them. When they got to the edge of the ravine where the truck was, the sheriff sent the deputy, Walt Mosley, down to retrieve the gun. Walt used a forked stick to pull the gun out by the trigger guard. When he got back to the top of the ravine, the sheriff held out a large paper envelope, and he dropped the gun in.

"Lawrs, why'd you come looking for the truck and gun?" the sheriff asked.

Lawrs didn't want to suggest the sheriff hadn't searched everything around the house and farm, so he said he thought someone might have overlooked the farrowing sheds. When he was out there, he said, he saw the ravine and decided it might be worth walking back there.

The sheriff said. "The way things are going, I should be able to wrap this up pretty fast. We'll get the revolver to the lab in Des Moines to see if there are prints. The lab can run a ballistics test to see if the bullet that killed the uncle came from that gun. Ten to one we'll find Martinek's fingerprints on it."

"Sheriff," Lawrs said, "I don't want to get anyone into any trouble, but I should probably tell you that Bill Robinson, who owns the land on the other side of the ravine"—he pointed in the direction of Robinson's farm— "hired Roy Mortensen to check the boundaries of his property. Apparently, he and Truesdale had several heated arguments about where the boundary was between their two places. At one point, they both drew guns."

Lawrs didn't want to pull Jim into the conversation, but Jim volunteered. "They've had other arguments, and it might have been Robinson I overheard fighting with Truesdale."

Lawrs explained his theory of how the crime might have been committed by Robinson. The sheriff looked skeptical; he had the kind of expression on his face that people have when they believe someone is definitely wrong. The corners of his mouth were down, his head was slightly tipped and turned, and he had one eyebrow higher than the other. As Lawrs knew, it wasn't easy to redirect the sheriff's thinking once he had made up his mind—and he was convinced that Martinek was the killer.

"I'll go have a talk with him. I'll ask him if he knew there was a truck back here. Hard to believe he didn't, but that doesn't mean he killed anybody."

The sheriff left just as the school bus arrived and the two Ross children got off. They came running to the house, wanting to know why the sheriff was there, again.

Their father just told them that they were back checking on things and let it go at that. Lawrs walked to the house with them.

When they were inside, to try to take their attention off the sheriff and the discoveries on Truesdale's property, Lawrs asked Tim, who was eight, "Tim, why does your sister jump up and down when she drinks her medicine?"

Not quite sure what Lawrs was up to, Tim said, "I don't know, why?"

Lawrs answered, "Because the directions on the bottle said to shake it well."

Tim looked at Lawrs with a completely straight face and asked, "Who's there?"

Playing along, Lawrs responded, "I don't know, who's there?"

"Hurd," Tim responded.

"Hurd who?" Lawrs said.

"Hurd my hand, so I couldn't knock, knock."

"Where did you get that joke?" Shirley asked, laughing.

"On the school bus," Tim said.

Not to be outdone, Tim's sister, Julie, who was six, asked, "How do you keep a dog in the back seat from barking?"

Lawrs, not expecting another comeback joke, especially from Julie, said, "I don't know, how do you keep a dog in the back seat from barking?"

"Put him in the front seat," Julie said. She added, "I got that on the bus, too."

"Lawrs, you'd better start riding the school bus," Jim said. "Otherwise you're going to be replaced."

Everyone laughed.

Chapter Eighteen

Friday, September 12, 1952

As Lawrs headed home, he decided his news was too good not to share. He would stop by Midway, tell Mac, ask her to call Stoner, and then drive to Belle Plaine to tell the guys over there.

When he got to Midway about three o'clock, he found Mac sitting at her usual place. She was excited to hear the news about the gun and the pickup, and she complimented Lawrs on his persistence.

Ruthie was just as excited. "Oh, Lawrs, they should elect you sheriff. You should run next time there is an election."

"Thanks, Ruthie, but I wouldn't be any good at being sheriff."

"Good at it?" she responded. "You found the body, you found the gun, you found the pickup—the sheriff didn't find anything. You'd be great. Mac can be your campaign manager, and I'll help."

"She's got a point, Lawrs," Mac said dryly. "The sheriff has to retire sometime."

"No, that doesn't interest me, but I appreciate your sentiments."

Ruthie was pleased to be been part of the discussion. Usually she worked behind the counter while everyone else sat at the Rounders' table and talked. She always felt a bit left out.

Lawrs then drove to Belle Plaine. It was almost four o'clock. He first stopped at Roy's. He wasn't there. Gene Hughes, Roy's next-door neighbor was in his yard. Lawrs went over and asked if he had seen Roy.

"No, I haven't," Hughes said. "I just got home from school about an hour ago, and I haven't seen him; I can't even remember seeing him yesterday."

"Maybe he's at Pansy's. He spends a lot of time down there doesn't he?" Lawrs asked.

"He sure does. If you don't find him, I'll tell him that you were looking for him when I do see him."

"Thanks a lot," Lawrs said. He headed for Pansy's garage. In a town the size of Belle Plaine, that wasn't too far away, just two blocks. He decided to walk.

When he got to Pansy's, he immediately told him about the gun and the pickup. Naturally, Pansy wanted to know where he had found it. Lawrs told him. He also explained his theory about Robinson.

When he got to the end of his story and Pansy had run out of questions, Lawrs asked: "I went by Roy's to tell him the news, but he wasn't there; do you know where he is?"

"No, he usually drops by every afternoon like clockwork." He looked at his watch. "He's over due. I drove him back from Midway yesterday, but I haven't seen him since. Let me call Fritz; sometimes he goes over there. Besides, he'll be glad to know about the gun and the pickup."

In Belle Plaine, there was a central telephone exchange with a full time operator and switchboard. You just asked for the number you wanted, and she connected you. Lawrs wondered if they'd ever get that kind of service in rural areas. Fritz answered after the first ring.

"Fritz? Pansy."

Before Pansy could tell him about Lawrs' discovery or the fact that Roy was missing, Fritz spoke up, "Pansy, I'm glad you called.

They've let Martinek out of jail. The county attorney decided they couldn't hold him any longer."

"That's interesting, Fritz, but I've got something even better. Lawrs just found the gun that probably killed Truesdale's uncle. It was in a ravine that runs along the back of his farm. The dark blue pickup was there, too; it had Ohio plates. The gun was in plain sight on the front seat."

"Wow!" Fritz said. "How did that happen?"

"Here, Lawrs," Pansy said, handing him the phone. "He wants to know what happened. You tell him."

Lawrs got on the phone and quickly ran through the story. When he finished, he said, "A few minutes ago, I went by Roy's to tell him the news, but he wasn't there. Pansy hasn't seen him. Hughes, his next-door neighbor, hasn't seen him today—or even yesterday. Have you seen him?"

"No, I haven't, and if Pansy hasn't seen him since yesterday, then that is strange."

After Lawrs had hung up, he and Pansy continued to talk about Roy's disappearance.

"I'm sure there's a logical explanation," Pansy said. "Maybe he's sick or something. He might have fallen. Let's check the place out."

"Good idea," Lawrs said. "I wouldn't want him lying on the floor of his house or in the yard, not able to call someone."

They walked the two blocks to Roy's house. The first thing they did was to search the yard. It wasn't particularly large, and there were no tall bushes that he could have fallen behind.

"Let's check in the house," Pansy suggested.

Walking toward the backdoor of Roy's house, Pansy said, "He never locks the place, so we won't have much trouble getting in."

The door opened easily, and they went in. As they looked around, Lawrs, who never been inside Roy's house, was startled by the piles of newspapers. They were standing everywhere, stacked throughout the house.

As they looked around, there was an unpleasant odor. The thought that instantly ran through Lawrs' mind was the smell in the chicken coop, but his was different.

A cat came up to Pansy and rubbed against his leg. Pansy said, "This is Saint, Roy's cat. He usually stays outside. I'm pretty sure the odor I'm smelling means he's had an accident in here."

As they looked further and went on to the living room, they passed the door to the bedroom. "The smell is coming from in there," Pansy said. He went inside. The place was a disaster. It was always a mess, but the bedclothes had been pulled off the bed, and a couple of the stacks of newspapers were scattered all over the floor. They could see Saint's accident.

"This isn't good, Pansy said. "There must have been a fight or something." He pointed to a chair beside the bed, "Those are the clothes he was wearing yesterday at Midway, and he doesn't change very often."

They searched the rest of the house; they even went upstairs to the two rooms on the second floor, rooms that Roy never used. They found nothing, except more boxes full of papers.

"This isn't good," Pansy repeated.

"No, I agree," Lawrs responded. He suddenly had an idea. "Maybe a client came by, and they drove over to Vinton in the client's car."

"That's possible," Pansy said. "But, that doesn't explain the mess in the bedroom, or the fact the cat was in."

Lawrs suggested, "Maybe we should call the sheriff. What with two murders already, he might want to know."

They used Roy's phone to call the sheriff. Once they got hold of him, Lawrs told the sheriff that Roy was missing and why they were concerned.

"You're really in the thick of things, aren't you young man?" the sheriff said with hostility in his voice.

"Just trying to do my duty," Lawrs said as politely as he could.

"I wouldn't worry too much. Let's wait a couple of days. If he hasn't shown up by then, call me again. We don't act on missing persons for a few days; more often than not, they show up on their own."

Lawrs wasn't happy with that answer, but when he persisted, the sheriff held his ground. He reminded the sheriff there had been two murders and that there were at least two men who might have had some reason for confronting Roy—Martinek and Robinson. The sheriff didn't budge. He was clearly annoyed at having received the call—especially from Lawrs.

After he had hung up, he told Pansy what the sheriff had said. Pansy wasn't happy with his response either. "I don't know what else we can do," Pansy said. "Lawrs, you go on home; I know you've got to get back for your evening chores. I'll feed Saint and make sure he's out."

Roy was gone, and his friends were worried. People didn't just go missing in small towns. Everybody knew everyone. If you weren't where you were supposed to be, people noticed, and they talked about it. Very little went undetected. It was both a blessing and a curse.

Chapter Nineteen

Saturday, September 13, 1952

After he was through with his morning chores, Lawrs drove over to Pansy's. It was Saturday, about eleven; Pansy kept the garage open Saturday mornings and usually closed Wednesday afternoons.

"Have you heard from Roy?" Lawrs asked as he walked into Pansy's office.

"No, I went over there before I came to work. He hasn't been there since we were there yesterday. His bed hasn't been slept in, and the cat's still outside. Something's wrong, but there's no point calling the sheriff again; he's already said he won't do anything."

Lawrs said, "His disappearance might have something to do with Robinson."

"You told me about him yesterday, but go over it again so I can understand your logic," Pansy said.

"Sure." Lawrs explained in an abbreviated, staccato manner: "Robinson has the farm behind Truesdale's. There is a ravine between the two places—the one where I found the uncle's pickup and the gun. Robinson thought he owned a small chunk of land on the same side of the ravine as Truesdale's property. He wants to fence it off for cattle. According to a neighbor, Jim Ross, they fought over the boundary several times—once with guns. Robinson asked Roy to go to Vinton to identify where the property line runs. Roy said Thursday he had gone to Vinton and the property line was where Robinson thought it was. Roy was going to tell Robinson that yesterday."

Lawrs continued, "Here's my theory: He goes to tell Robinson what he had found in Vinton. Out of curiosity, Roy walks out to see where the line is. He spots the pickup; he recognizes it from Pansy's description. Robinson sees him, and he has to do something to keep Roy from reporting the pickup and connecting him to the killings."

"Makes sense, except for one thing," Pansy said, "Roy doesn't have a car; he had no way to get to Robinson's."

"I forgot." Lawrs paused. "Isn't there some other way he could have gotten there? What if he hitched a ride with somebody—like a delivery guy? Maybe he figured Robinson would be happy about the property line, and he would be willing to bring him home. I know I'm grasping at straws," Lawrs added. "But there has got to be some explanation."

"Here's a twist on your theory," Pansy said. "Let's suppose you're right: Roy caught a ride to Martinek's, went out to see the property line, and saw the truck. But here's the twist: Remember, Fritz told us yesterday they let Martinek out. If he killed Truesdale and his uncle, he would have been the one who drove the truck into the ravine. Suppose he went over to Truesdale's to get the truck and dispose of it. When he was there, Roy saw him, and Martinek silenced him so he wouldn't tell people.

"Maybe," Lawrs said. "But Robinson would have gone out with him, and he didn't get killed. I still think it's Robinson."

Both men were quiet for a short time. Finally, Pansy said, "All we know is that Roy is missing, and we need to find him. Let's call the other Rounders and get them over here; together, we can check all the places in Belle Plaine where he might have walked. We'll also go see Robinson. We'll tell him that we knew Roy was supposed to see him yesterday and ask him if he showed up. Maybe he'll trip himself up somehow."

Lawrs agreed. Within forty minutes, Fritz, Mac, and Stoner had arrived.

Pansy started. "Let's be sure we all know the same things." He explained that they couldn't find Roy and that the sheriff wouldn't help. He told them about the signs of a scuffle in Roy's bedroom. He asked Lawrs to explain his theory about Robinson.

When Lawrs was done, Fritz told them that Martinek had been released. Pansy explained his alternative theory about how Martinek might have been in involved in Roy's disappearance.

Stoner had one comment about the fact that the sheriff had let Martinek out of jail: "Damn the incompetent son-of-a-bitch, and damn him for not looking for Roy." No one, including Mac, commented on her language.

Pansy continued, "Let's go to every store downtown to see if anyone has seen Roy. It's Saturday, and there will be lots of people in town. Fritz, you, Stoner, and Mac take Main Street and the businesses along Thirteenth Street. One of you should stop at the police station. That's about thirty-five or forty places altogether. You can cover them pretty fast if you break up and each take ten or so."

He went on, "Lawrs and I will drive down by the railroad tracks to where Roy's old corncob factory was—just in case he went there and fell or something. Then, we'll drive to Robinson's and see what he says. Lawrs could go alone since he knows him, but I think that there ought to be two of us when we talk to Robinson." People nodded their heads in agreement. "Let's plan to meet back here about four. If we still haven't found him, we can we decide what we'll do next."

Pansy and Lawrs left for Roy's old factory. Mac, Stoner, and Fritz divided things up and started canvassing the town. They agreed they would just say they were in town, had an appointment with Roy, couldn't find him, and wondered if anyone had seen him.

Along the way, Fritz went into the telephone exchange and asked the operator on duty if she had gotten or received any calls to or from Roy in the last two days. She could remember placing a call to Robinson—she thought it was Thursday. She said that he made a second call, but she couldn't remember to whom. She checked with the night operator and the relief operator. They couldn't remember any call—to or from Roy.

Pansy and Lawrs stopped at the edge of town and walked the railroad tracks to the abandoned building Roy had built as part of his scheme to turn corncobs into plastic.

First, they walked around the outside of the building. Then, they struggled to pull the door open. The shaft of the building went up two stories. As they entered, they could see bats at the top of the shaft. The noise of the door had startled them, and some flew out the broken windows near the roof.

Inside, the floor was covered with coal dust. The steam locomotives at the roundhouse a couple of hundred yards away had spewed it out over the last couple of decades. They concluded that no one had been there for years.

Then, they drove to Robinson's. Pansy had never met him.

When they got there, he was in the barn behind his house. He was shoveling manure into a spreader with a pitchfork. He had been sweating and had his shirt off; he was a large, strong man. The smell of manure was pungent. "Hi, Bill," Lawrs said; he introduced Pansy. "We're looking for Roy Mortensen. Have you seen him? He told me Thursday he was going to come to see you about the property line issue he was helping you with. Has he been here?"

"No, he called me on the phone Thursday afternoon and told me that everything was the way I thought it was."

Hoping to get more out of him, Lawrs asked, “Did you know about the sheriff finding Truesdale’s uncle’s car in the ravine?”

“You bet. He came over here. Some discovery, uh, Lawrs—Jim told me that you were the one who really found it. I don’t know why I didn’t see it, but I don’t go back there very often.”

“When he called you, did Roy tell you where he was or give you any indication of what he might be going to do later?” Pansy asked.

“He said he was calling me from his house. We didn’t talk about anything except the property line. He didn’t say a thing about what he planned to do later.”

Lawrs glanced at Pansy to see if he thought there was anything else that they should ask. Pansy shrugged his shoulders slightly, and then Lawrs said, “Thanks Bill, sorry to bother you. We just haven’t been able to find Roy since yesterday, and we’re concerned. If you see him or hear from him, would you call me?”

“Oh, sure, you’re on the Newhall exchange aren’t you?” Lawrs nodded his head, and Bill offered, “I hope nothing has happened to him.”

Lawrs and Pansy said goodbye and got in their car. “That was a dead end,” Pansy said.

“Yeah, I guess I was pretty naïve,” Lawrs responded. “You wouldn’t expect him to give himself away.”

When everyone reassembled at Pansy’s office, it was just after four o’clock. They reported on what each of them had and had not found. Fritz told them that the daytime telephone exchange operator remembered placing a call from Roy to Robinson. “Yes, that’s what Robinson told us,” Lawrs said.

“She also said he placed a second call, but she couldn’t remember to whom.”

They discussed what they should do next. After considering several options, Lawrs and Pansy offered to go to Vinton to see the sheriff in person; they said they would enlist Samuelson's help. They thought the sheriff wouldn't be quite so quick to dismiss his concerns.

Before they broke up, Fritz suggested that he would go to Roy's house and look through his business papers and notes. Maybe, he said, he could find something that would give them a clue to his whereabouts. They all agreed that would be a good idea.

Pansy and Lawrs took separate cars to Vinton because they would need to take different routes to get back to their respective homes; Lawrs needed to get home as soon as he could to do his evening chores.

Everyone was worried. Roy was a good friend and a kind man. He wasn't the sort to get himself in a situation where someone might go after him.

Chapter Twenty

Late Afternoon, Saturday, September 12, 1952.

Lawrs and Pansy agreed to meet Samuelson' office. It was just before five o'clock when they met, and they hoped he would be in his office. They were in luck. The door wasn't locked, and they went in.

Lawrs greeted the young receptionist on duty. "Hey, Claire, how are you doing? It's been a long time since I've seen you."

She responded, "Yes, Lawrs, it has been a long time. I was beginning to think you'd dropped off the map. It's good to see you're still around." There was some sarcasm in her voice.

"Claire, this is Frank O'Malley from Belle Plaine. Is Mr. Samuelson in? We know it's late, but we'd like to see him if he's here. Tell him it's about Roy Mortensen; it's important."

"Well, let me see if he's busy. I know you don't have an appointment," she said rather coolly. She went down the hall to Samuelson' office.

After she had gone, Pansy turned to Lawrs and said, "Do you know every single girl in the county, Lawrs?"

"I guess," he grinned, "and some that aren't single."

The receptionist came back and said a bit testily, "He can see you. Come this way."

When they entered Samuelson' office, the lawyer stood up, motioned to the two chairs in front of his desk, and said, "Gentlemen, sit down. What can I do to help you? It's something important about Roy Mortensen?"

Lawrs started, "We wouldn't bother you, Mr. Samuelson, but Roy has been missing for two days. We know he comes over to Vinton every once in a while, and we know he's a friend of yours. We thought you might have seen him."

He continued, "We came over to ask your opinion about what we should do. We talked to the sheriff yesterday, but he said we should wait a few days to be sure he doesn't come back on his own. We'd go back to the sheriff, but we don't think he would listen to us."

Samuelson responded, "Roy and I went to school together back east, so we know each other well. I saw him on Monday; tell me what's happened since."

The two men took turns telling him what they knew. It was clear that Samuelson was concerned by what they said, including the connection with both Martinek and Robinson. They asked him what they should do next.

"I don't think we should waste any time," Samuelson said, "I'll try to get the sheriff. He doesn't come to the courthouse on Saturdays, but he's usually willing to help on weekends if it's important."

Samuelson called the sheriff's home number. When he answered, Samuelson apologized for calling on the weekend, but he explained what Pansy and Lawrs had told him.

Although the sheriff was not happy to be called at suppertime, let alone on the weekend, he agreed to meet them at his office in the courthouse within half an hour. Lawrs and Pansy stayed in Samuelson' office until then.

It was about six o'clock by the time the sheriff arrived. His office was entered from a ground level, outside door at the side of the building; he didn't have a key to the front doors. He unlocked the door and let them in.

After they all had been seated, Lawrs began. "Sheriff, I know I called you on Friday, but Roy didn't show up again today. We think something has happened to him. He hasn't slept in his house for two nights, and there are indications in the house that there might have been a fight."

Lawrs continued, "We thought he might have had a heart attack or something, so we searched his yard, too."

Pansy continued the story, "Early this afternoon, five of us went door to door to all the stores in Belle Plaine asking people if they had seen him. Lawrs and I even went to the old factory he built a dozen years or so ago. We couldn't find him, and no one we talked to had seen him. We even drove out to see Bill Robinson, the man Lawrs told you about yesterday. He hadn't seen him either."

Lawrs took over, "I know you told us to wait, but we know Roy pretty well, and we're convinced something has happened. We hoped he would show up and be okay, but he's definitely missing. We need your help."

Samuelson spoke up, "Lawrs and Frank told me all this when they came to see me a few minutes ago, and I am in agreement with them, sheriff. Something has happened to Roy. Can you do anything to help us?"

The sheriff wasn't as inclined to be as negative with Samuelson as he had been with Lawrs. He said, "It sounds as though you've done almost everything anyone could think of doing. I don't know what more I can do but put out a missing person bulletin. I wouldn't know where to begin a physical search for him that you haven't already tried."

Samuelson said they would appreciate whatever he could do.

The sheriff continued, "I'll tell you what, gentlemen. I agree something suspicious is going on. I might not say that if we hadn't had two murders and two robberies in the last couple of weeks."

"That concerns us too," Lawrs said. "We are afraid his disappearance has something to do with the murders."

The sheriff continued, "I'll put out the missing person's bulletin tonight. On Monday, I'll go around to the places in Vinton he might have gone; you can go with me if you want to, Everett. I'll also call the highway patrol."

"He doesn't have a car," Pansy said, "so it will be hard for the patrol to know what to do." The sheriff agreed, but he said he would call them anyway.

Roy's three friends were disappointed, but they couldn't think of what else to ask the sheriff to do. They had no choice but to wait until Monday and hope that some clue to Roy's disappearance would turn up before then.

After they had left the sheriff's office, the three men stood talking. Samuelson said, "I know that you're unhappy with the way the sheriff left things; I am too. But, it's probably the best we can do; I've learned the hard way you can't push him. He just digs in harder and refuses to act. I'll keep on his case and let you know what he does."

"We appreciate that," Lawrs said; Pansy agreed.

"I'll give you my home phone number in case something comes up; don't hesitate to call no matter what time it is. Roy's a good friend, and I'm as concerned as you are. Will you give me your numbers?" Samuelson asked.

After the men had exchanged phone numbers, they got into their separate cars, each heading home. It was almost seven o'clock. The sun had already set.

That night on the ten o'clock news, the WMT newscaster announced: "The sheriff of Benton County has issued a missing-persons report for a man from Belle Plaine. His name is Roy Mortensen. Mr. Mortensen is a well-known lawyer and horticulturist in that town. He has been missing for two days. Mr. Mortensen is believed to be about 68. He is a small man who usually wears charcoal-gray flannel slacks, dress shirts without a tie, and a Panama hat. The sheriff asks anyone who knows anything about Mr. Mortensen's disappearance to call his office in Vinton."

Chapter Twenty-one

Saturday Evening, September 12, 1952.

Roy woke up with a throbbing headache. It took a few minutes to focus. Where was he? It was a strange place he didn't recognize. Immediately, he felt pain in his arms and feet. They were bound, and he had been tied to a cot. How had he gotten into this situation? He couldn't remember.

He wasn't gagged, so he did what most people would do under the circumstances: he started yelling for help. After three or four minutes, his throat was getting tense, and he recognized that either no one could hear him, or no one was willing to help. He was thirsty; his mouth was dry.

He remained quiet for a while. As he did, his memory gradually began to return. It was last night. Was he sure it was last night? Had he been here longer? All he could remember was that he had been in bed at home, and someone had attacked him.

He remembered he fought back, but the other person, it seemed like a man, was stronger than he was; he was on top of him, holding him down. The person must have hit him on the head, and he blacked out. He knew nothing that had happened between that moment and now. He did sense a swollen lump on his head, even though he couldn't touch it, and he could see blood on his clothes.

Why was he here? Who had done this? He could not think of a reason why anyone would have attacked him. Was it a burglary? Was there anything in his house of value? He could think of nothing anyone would want. He could burn the place down, and no one would care.

Surely his ex-wife wouldn't arrange anything like this. They certainly weren't on good terms when they separated. They hadn't spoken to each other in years. How could his death help her? Would she have taken out an insurance policy on his life? She was so vindictive, he wouldn't put it past her—but that was ridiculous—no insurance company would issue a policy for an ex-husband without an interview or a physical examination.

He mentally went through a list of people he knew in an attempt to try to identify anyone who would do this.

The first name that came to him was that of Lawrs. Why? He liked Lawrs, and he thought Lawrs liked him. Mac? She had no reason to be angry with him.

Stoner? Fritz?

He didn't know Stoner well, but what reason could she have to hurt him? It was a man who attacked him anyway—he was pretty sure. Fritz had been his friend for a long time; he wouldn't do something like this. The same was true for Pansy; he was his best friend. They had spent many an hour arguing over world affairs, politics, and the economy.

He rambled through a list of other people. What about Martinek? He didn't know Martinek. What reason would he have for wanting Roy dead? He was in jail anyway.

Robinson? He knew Robinson at least, and he remembered that Robinson had fought with Truesdale and that guns had been involved. But that had nothing to do with Roy. The only thing he'd done for Robinson was check on his property line; he hadn't found anything that would give Robinson a reason to be angry.

The only conclusion he could come to was that it was an entirely random act: kids wanting to see how far they could go in scaring an old man or a complete lunatic who had some deep-seated mental problem. Yes, that made more sense.

He began to pay attention to the room around him. It was obviously in an old house. It smelled dusty, and there was a distinct odor of mold in the air. The old wallpaper was falling off. There were two windows, boarded up and covered with faded, torn, muslin curtains. Very little light crept through the cracks in the boards, but he could tell it was daylight outside.

There were two doors. If this were a dining room, one of them would lead to the living room and the other to the kitchen. If it were a living room, it would have an outside door. There would be a sill; the door would close at the bottom so that it didn't let in rain or snow. That was not the case for either of these two doors; he could see an inch or more clearance under both of them.

The room was empty except for a chair, a small wooden table against one of the walls, and the cot he was tied to. He looked up; there was a single light receptacle hanging from a cord coming down from the ceiling, but there was no bulb. Even if there had been a bulb, he guessed, there wouldn't be any electricity in a place like this. It was already getting dark. Spending the night in total darkness would be awful, Roy thought.

Where was this place?

He guessed it wasn't in a small town; the neighbors would get suspicious. What made the most sense to him was that it was an abandoned farmhouse.

He suddenly heard a noise. It sounded like a car. He could hear it get closer. He recognized the sound that gravel made when a car ran over it.

The car stopped. The next sound was a door opening. It must have been an outside door in the next room. The door closed; he could hear footsteps coming across the wooden floor toward the room he was in.

He heard and saw the knob on the door turn. A muffled voice said, "You'd better be tied up on the cot when I come in, old man. I have a gun; if you attack me, I'll shoot you. Do you hear me?" the voice asked.

"Yes, I hear you," Roy said, "I'm still tied to this damned bed. Untie me." Suddenly he became self-conscious. He realized he'd been tied up so long that he had wet his nightclothes. It hadn't even occurred to him until now that he was even in his nightclothes.

What difference did that make? Under the circumstances, it didn't matter.

The door slowly opened. A figure stood in the doorway. There was light coming from behind him, presumably from a window in the next room that was not boarded up. What Roy noticed immediately was that he had a mask on; it completely covered his face. It was like one of those masks that members of the Ku Klux Klan wore, with slits for the eyes and mouth—except it wasn't pointed; it conformed to the man's head.

He wore nondescript clothes: old khakis and a checkered shirt. His shoes were older, scuffed and heavy, almost like a boot; the kind most farmers wore. But the most noticeable thing, besides the hood, was the shotgun that the man pointed at him.

Was it Martinek? Had they let him go? He had never met him, so he wouldn't have known his voice.

Roy spoke up. "What do you want? Why have you done this? Where am I?"

The man spoke gruffly, trying to change his voice so Roy couldn't recognize him. "I don't have to tell you anything, but I'm going to let you live until I can decide what to do with you."

"I'm hungry and thirsty. I need something to eat and drink," Roy demanded. "At least let me stand up."

"I'm not going to risk that. I've brought some food and water; I'll untie you enough so you can sit up and eat a little." He went back into the other room and brought back a metal cup with a handle; across the top of the cup was a sandwich. He still had the gun in the other hand. He put it down long enough to untie Roy's hands and the ropes that held his upper body. He handed Roy the cup and sandwich. "Here, eat." He picked the shotgun back up.

Roy was hungry; he quickly ate the sandwich and drank all of the water in the cup.

"How long are you going to keep me here? Where am I?"

The muffled voice said, "Like I said, I haven't decided what to do with you. As to where you are, you're in an old abandoned house out in the country. No one is going to find you—even though your friends are looking for you. They've got the whole town of Belle Plaine upset. Even if I kill you, it may be a satisfaction for you to know that a lot of people care about you."

"How long have I been here?"

"You've been here since early Friday morning."

"What day is it now?"

"It's Saturday evening."

"Saturday? My God I've been here more than a day? Have I been out all that time?"

"Pretty much," the man answered.

"Oh, God! Please let me go! What have I ever done to you?" Roy begged.

"Get back down on the cot; I'm going to tie you back up."

"Please don't."

The man pushed Roy back on the cot. It didn't require much force; Roy was weak. He re-tied his upper body and hands. He then went to the door and placed his hand on the knob. Turning back to face Roy, he said, "Let's just say you know something I don't want other people to know. I'll be back in the morning. I'll bring some more food and water. I'll untie you then and let you move around. But you'd better still be tied up when I come back."

He closed the door behind him as he exited the room. Roy heard the door in the other room, the outside door, shut as well. Then he heard the sound of a car starting up and driving away across the gravel. It was almost completely dark.

This was beyond belief, Roy said to himself. Who could hate me this much? What in the world do I know that someone might not want other people to know? He mentally started going through a list of people again. And then, a person came to his mind. He knew who had kidnapped him.

Chapter Twenty-two

Early Morning, Sunday, September 14, 1952.

The same name that came to Roy's mind was on Fritz McKay's mind very early Sunday morning.

He immediately called Pansy. His wife answered; she had been asleep when the phone rang. Fritz asked to speak to Pansy, telling her that it was urgent.

As soon as Pansy said hello in a sleepy voice, Fritz leaped in, "Pansy, I think I know who might have taken Roy."

"Fritz? Is that you? What the hell time is it?"

"It's only—" he paused to look at his watch. "I'm sorry, it's about two o'clock. But this is important. I think I know who took Roy."

"Where are you?"

"I just got home; I've been going through papers at Roy's every since I saw you at your office."

"What did you find?"

"About half an hour ago I found a file folder that contained an important court document and a diagram Roy must have drawn."

He described the diagram, "In the upper left corner is the name, 'Sarah Caldwell.' A line runs straight down from her name to the name 'John Truesdale' at the bottom. In the upper right, are the names: 'Jake and Evelyn Winfield.' A line runs down from their names to the bottom where 'Sam Winfield' is written. But the most important thing is a diagonal line running from 'Sarah Caldwell' to 'Sam Winfield.'"

"I don't get it," Pansy said.

"The court document explains it."

"What kind of document is it?"

"It's from a district judge for Benton County. I won't read it, but the gist is that the judge was releasing the adoption records for Sam Winfield—I didn't even know he was adopted. His birth mother was Sarah Caldwell, and his adopted parents were Jake and Evelyn Winfield. It still didn't quite registered with me until I remembered that Roy had said John Truesdale's mother's maiden name was Caldwell, the same as his uncle. If Sarah Caldwell is the mother of both John Truesdale and Sam Winfield, we've got a real connection between the two of them: they are half-brothers."

"Wow!" Pansy said. "That's incredible. Listen, that connects with something Roy told me Thursday. He asked how well I knew Winfield. I said I had only just met him at the Rounders' meetings. He said he'd done some legal work for Winfield, but didn't say what it was. It must have been getting the court to release Winfield's adoption records. I'm not sure what it means about Roy's disappearance, though."

Fritz suggested, "Let's just suppose Winfield had something to do with Truesdale's death and maybe his uncle's. He wouldn't want anyone to know about the connection. Roy knows about it, and he doesn't want Roy to talk—so he kidnaps him and is holding him—or worse."

"I hate to think about that."

"What should we do? Call the sheriff?"

"Lawrs and I saw him last night, but all he would do was to put out a missing person's bulletin. Let me call Samuelson; he was with us. It's awfully early, but he gave us his home telephone number in case something developed. He's a good friend of Roy's, and he said we could call him anytime. Let me tell him. He may be able to get the sheriff to act."

"Yeah, but don't tell him how I got the information; he might be upset that I was going through Roy's confidential legal papers." He paused, "Hell, I don't care what you tell him, just do it."

Pansy hung up and called Samuelson. It was a two-thirty in the morning when he got through.

"Everett, I'm sorry to call you so early. I know what time it is, but I think I've figured out what's happened to Roy. On our way home from the last Rounders' meeting, Roy said he'd done some legal work for Sam Winfield—he's a postman and delivers Truesdale's mail. He just started coming to the Rounders' meetings—sitting in on our discussions about Truesdale."

He continued without fully revealing his source of information: "I just found out that the work Roy did for Winfield was to petition the district court to open his adoption records. He found out that Winfield's natural mother was Sarah Caldwell. Then I remembered that when Roy went to Vinton recently, he found out that John Truesdale's mother's maiden name was Sarah Caldwell."

What he said next startled Samuelson, "That makes Winfield and Truesdale half-brothers. If Winfield killed Truesdale, Winfield knows Roy might have figured it out. He'd have to keep Roy quiet so he—well, I don't want to think about what he might have done. Will this get the sheriff to act?"

"I think so. We just have to prove to him what you've figured out. He won't act on my word alone, and he won't accept your word for it either. We have to have written proof, and I can get it here in Vinton with help from the clerk of the court and the county clerk. Leave it to me, but it may take a few hours. I won't call the sheriff right now; it's too early. It might antagonize him if I call now, but I know he's an early riser. I'll call him about six. I know we should do it right now, but we need the sheriff on our side. He's the only one who can persuade the courthouse folks to open their offices on a Sunday. They're the only ones who'll have access to the documentation that proves what you've explained. I'll get back to you after I talk to the sheriff."

After he had hung up, Samuelson tried to go back to sleep, but he couldn't; his mind was running through the details of what he had heard. Experiences they shared from their time at Harvard also entered his thoughts. He just couldn't sleep.

At six o'clock, he called the sheriff's home.

"Ralph, this is Everett Samuelson, I'm sorry to bother you at home so early on Sunday, but this is important. We think we know what's happened to Roy Mortensen—it involves kidnapping or murder. I need your help."

"What?" the sheriff said. "What are you talking about?"

"Just hear me out, Ralph. That man in your office yesterday evening, Frank O'Malley, called me a few minutes ago. He told me about a conversation he had with Roy on Thursday. Roy told him that he was working on an adoption case for a man named Sam Winfield. Winfield was adopted, and he wanted to try to find the names of his birth parents. He needed Roy to get the court to unseal his adoption records. The bottom line is that Roy found out that Sam Winfield and John Truesdale are half-brothers. We think that puts Winfield in the picture for the murder of Truesdale and his uncle. We believe Winfield has at least kidnapped Roy—if not something worse, so he can't say anything that would tie him back to the two murders."

"Who's Winfield?" the sheriff asked.

"He delivers mail around Midway."

"I'm listening," the sheriff said.

"I know I need to prove all of this to you, Ralph, but I can only do that if you can get the clerk of the court to verify that Sarah Caldwell is Winfield's natural mother. We need the county clerk to confirm that she's also the mother of Truesdale. I know you could wait to confirm this at the courthouse Monday, but I'm afraid Roy is in mortal danger. With this information, you can solve two murders and prevent a third." He was mindful of the need to play to the sheriff's ego.

"You're probably right," the sheriff said, reluctantly. "I'll call the clerk and get him to open things up so we can look at the adoption records. I'll get someone in the recorder's office to check on birth certificates. There will be all hell to pay, getting them over to the courthouse on Sunday, but I agree with you. The last thing I need around here is another murder. I'll get the courthouse open, even if I have to call the district judge to make them do it. I know the clerk of the court is a lay-minister, so he won't be willing to come this morning. Meet me at the courthouse at two o'clock, and I'll unravel this thing."

It worked, Samuelson said to himself. He called Pansy.

A few minutes before two that afternoon, Samuelson waited at the door of the courthouse. The sheriff's car drove up, and he got out. The clerk of the court, a man named Philip Watson, got out along with Jessie Wilkins, from the county clerk's office.

As Watson opened the door to the courthouse with his key, he said, "Ralph, I hope you haven't got me out on some goose chase. I've never opened this place to anyone on a Sunday." Jessie Wilkins said nothing; she was at the bottom of the totem pole.

Watson opened the door to his office on the second floor and went over to the walk-in vault; naturally, it was locked. "In the big cities," Watson said, "courthouses and banks have timers on these vaults so you can't open them until certain times. You ought to be thankful this is an old courthouse and we don't have any fancy timers."

He knew the combination from memory. He turned the dial back and forth several times, and then he spun the wheel that retracted the huge bolts. The door was heavy; Samuelson helped him pull it open.

"Now," he asked, "what are we looking for?"

Samuelson answered, "The sheriff needs to see the adoption records for a Samuel Winfield. You should already have a petition to the court to open them. We want to verify that his birth mother is a woman named Sarah Caldwell."

"Yes, I remember. That lawyer fellow Roy Mortensen from Belle Plaine was in here with a petition to get the judge to open the records for Winfield. We sent them to him a couple of days ago."

That, Samuelson said to himself, explains the timing of things. Roy just received the records. That means he didn't know Winfield's mother's name or that Truesdale was his half-brother until then. Once he knew and told Winfield he knew, Winfield had to act. Now it made sense.

"Let me find them," Watson said. "There's not enough room for all of us in there, I'll bring them out." He turned on the light in the vault as he entered. In less than two minutes, he came back out.

Handing papers to the sheriff, he said, "Here they are."

The sheriff took them.

Samuelson said, "We want to see if Sam Winfield's mother's name is on the record."

The sheriff read through portions of the three-page document. "Right. Sam Winfield's birth mother's name was Caldwell, Sarah Caldwell. There is no father's name listed."

"That's all we need here," Samuelson said. "Now Jessie, can we go down to your office and see who Sarah Caldwell married and confirm that she is also the mother of John Truesdale?"

Watson took the papers back into the vault and came out. With Samuelson help, he closed the vault door, spun the wheel and then the combination lock.

They went down one floor to the county clerk's office.

Jessie pulled out her key. "I'm sorry you couldn't reach the county clerk himself, but he's out of town. I'm glad you could get hold of me. I know Roy, and I'm concerned about his disappearance."

She opened the door and went behind the counter to the vault. She also knew the combination from memory. She turned the dial and then the wheel that retracted the bolts. Samuelson helped her pull the door open.

She said, "It is tight in there, just like it is upstairs. Let me go in, and I'll bring out what you want. I'm looking for a marriage license between Sarah Caldwell and a man named Truesdale, right? This will only take a few minutes; thank heavens we have indexes."

She entered the vault. When she came out, she was holding a large book. She said, "Okay, you're in luck. Here's the record of a marriage between Sarah Caldwell and Ralph Truesdale. They were married on the fourth of February, 1924; the wedding was performed by a justice of peace here in Vinton."

"That's great," Samuelson said emphatically.

Jessie continued, "Now, you want Truesdale's birth certificate, right? Do you want Winfield's as well? Even though the adoption records are upstairs, we should have a birth certificate for him. His birth mother's name won't be on it, and it won't indicate he was adopted, but it will have the names of his adoptive parents."

"Right," Samuelson said, and then he added, "The sheriff will need true copies of all these records tomorrow. Is that a problem?" Both Watson and Wilkins agreed to provide them.

Wilkins took the large book she had brought out with Sarah's marriage in it and reentered the vault. Soon she brought out two more large books; she had placed pieces of paper in the books to mark the pages they wanted. She opened the first one and read: "John Truesdale was born on the third of March, 1925 to Sarah and Ralph Truesdale."

She handed that book to the sheriff and opened the second one. "Samuel Winfield was born on the thirteenth of January, 1921; his parents are shown as Jacob and Evelyn Winfield. Like I said earlier, we know those are his adoptive parents—even though it doesn't say that."

"Sheriff, have you got what you want?" Watson asked.

"One more thing while we're here," Samuelson said. "Jesse, can you give me a property address for Winfield?"

"Sure, just give me a minute." She went back in and used the index to the township maps to locate Winfield's address.

When she returned with it, Samuelson motioned for her to give it to the sheriff who said, "I've got everything I want, right?"

"Yes," he answered.

The sheriff helped Jessie carry the books back to the vault. When he came out he spoke to the two county officials, "Thank you both. Sorry to get you out on Sunday, but this will help me solve two murders, if not three. Lock up the vault Jessie, and I'll drive both of you home. Everett, do you want to come down to my office when I get back? I will decide what to do next."

"I'll be glad to," Samuelson said. "I'll be waiting for you."

Everyone left the courthouse; Watson locked the outside door. Watson and Wilkins got into the sheriff's car, and he took them home.

While he waited, Samuelson had time to reflect. The story was almost too bazaar to believe. Things like this didn't happen in Vinton County. At the same time, he knew they did. Under the veneer of a society that generally reflected middle class values and where violent crimes seldom occurred, there was an undercurrent of malevolence. People were not only petty, but they held deep-seated resentment and sometimes hatred for others. It didn't take much to crack the surface and display the rawness underneath. As a lawyer, he saw it every day. Money was frequently at the core of the problem. Someone wanted what someone else had; they thought they were entitled to it. When they didn't get what they thought they were due, aberrant behaviors emerged. Wills and estates, particularly, brought out the worst in people, including families that were otherwise close—or should have been.

IT DIDN'T TAKE TOO LONG for the sheriff to return from dropping the two courthouse employees at their homes. Samuelson was waiting outside and approached the sheriff as he opened the outside, ground-level door to his offices. They both went into his office.

"Everett, on the way back, I've decided to go to Winfield's place right away and bring him in for questioning. When I dropped Jessie off, I went into her house, called my deputy, and told him to get right over here. I'll go just as soon as he gets here. Do you want to come along?"

"I'll come if you want me to, but I'd just be someone else you'd have to worry with."

"Right. We can handle it. With any luck, we can have him in custody in a few hours. I'll try to get him to tell me where Roy is and rescue him—if it's not too late," he added, ominously. "I'll give you a ring and tell you what happened."

After the sheriff let Samuelson out of the office, he went across the street to his office to call Pansy. When he answered, Samuelson went through the events of the afternoon. He also mentioned his hypothesis that Roy's abduction had been triggered by the fact the court had just sent the adoption records to him. He said he believed that Roy had probably told Winfield what the records contained, causing him to act.

Before he hung up, Samuelson asked Pansy to call Lawrs. He did. Pansy called Fritz next, then Mac and Stoner. He told them what Samuelson had discovered; he added that the sheriff was going out to look for both Winfield and Roy.

They all hoped that Roy was okay, but, under the circumstances, they were even more worried than they had been before. They were very much afraid for their friend.

Chapter Twenty-three

Sunday Evening, September 14, 1952

As soon as Deputy Sheriff Walter Mosley arrived at the sheriff's office, they left for Winfield's farm.

It took awhile to find the house. They made a wrong turn at one point and had to stop and ask a farmer where they could find Winfield's house. The only way they knew it was his house when they got there was because his name was on the mailbox.

By this time, it was evening and everything was getting dark. Kretzler couldn't see Winfield's car, but there was a garage; if Winfield was at home, his car would probably be in the garage. He looked. There was no car inside. The house was dark. He decided to try the front door first.

He used the same method that he and deputy Moseley had used to take Clyde Martinek into custody. The sheriff went to the door with his gun drawn while the deputy stood out in the yard with his gun. For all Kretzler knew, Winfield would resist arrest as Martinek had; he didn't want to take any chances.

He knocked loudly on the door. A dog barked inside. He waited a short time and knocked again. No light came on, and there was no other sound from inside. The third time he knocked very loudly and yelled Winfield's name. The dog continued barking. There was still no response. He tried the door. It was locked.

The sheriff turned to his deputy and said, "Let's go around the house and see if the back door is open."

They went to the backdoor. There was a screen door leading to a small porch. The screen was not hooked, and they entered the porch; the sheriff walked over to the door of the house. "Walt, keep your gun out. I'll try the door." With his gun in one hand, he used the other to open the door.

As soon as it opened, a large yellow dog ran toward him. Not knowing his name, Kretzler just said, "Good boy, good boy." The dog started wagging his tail. The sheriff reached out and patted him on the head.

It was dark in the house. The sheriff felt along the wall of the room near the door and found a light switch. The deputy joined him as soon as he saw the light come on. They were in the kitchen.

The sheriff called out again, announcing their presence.

The kitchen was neat although somewhat old fashioned. A large sink hung on the wall; it was a single piece of porcelain with drain boards molded on both sides. The stove was a combination propane gas and wood-burning range.

Turning on lights as they went, they walked through to the dining room. The dog followed their every move. This must have been the room where Winfield spent most of the time. The dining table was pushed against the wall with chairs drawn up under it. There was an overstuffed chair and a magazine rack; in the corner was a small black and white television set with rabbit ears on top. Beyond was the living room; it contained a sofa, a matching chair, and a platform rocker; the room didn't look as though it was used.

They went back to the dining room. There was a small hall to one side. It accessed the stairs to the second story and a half bath downstairs. The sheriff called upstairs; no one answered.

The dog was ahead of them at this point, and he went up the stairs. Hearing nothing except the dog's nails on the wooden floor above, the sheriff went up, followed by his deputy. The stairs squeaked as they ascended.

There were two bedrooms on the upper floor, one in the front and one in the back.

There was a small bathroom between them; you faced it as you reached the top of the stairs. The sheriff stuck his head inside; there was a claw-footed tub, sink, stool, and nothing else.

They went to the front bedroom next. It was obvious that Winfield did not use the room. It had a chenille spread on the bed, a chest of drawers, and a closet. He opened the closet and found only a couple of boxes of clothes. There was a strong smell of mothballs inside.

The back bedroom was the same, although there was no bedspread on the bed, just a quilt. The room was neat, however, and the bed had been made. Winfield's clothes were in the closet, and there was no detectable mothball smell.

"He sure isn't here," Kretzler said. "Let's check the outbuildings."

The sun had set, and there was less than a quarter moon; they had to use their flashlights.

The machine shed was open on one side. There was a small tractor and a wagon under the roof on the open side. Behind, was a door that led to a toolroom. Kretzler said to Mosley, "We need to keep our eye out for a body, a gun, or blood. He might have brought Mortensen here."

They searched the tool room and found nothing. Next, they went into the barn. It was small, with only three milking stalls on the main level. There was a place for a few calves on the other side and a loft. Hoping not to find a body, they looked in the stalls, including the feed troughs.

The sheriff said, "Walt, you go up to the loft and look around. I don't do ladders well at my age."

The deputy, who had said almost nothing since they arrived at the farm, simply responded, "Sure, sheriff." Every few minutes he would call down to report he had found nothing unusual. He was reasonably thorough. He used a pitchfork to poke into the loose hay, but most of it was bailed and easy to examine. He came down.

There was an old out-house behind the house, and they checked that.

It was almost ten by this time. "Well, I guess we've done everything we can," Kretzler said. "Let's go home, and we'll get on this again in the morning. I'll have to think about where we can look for either Winfield or Mortensen."

Deputy Moseley said, "What time do you want me to come in tomorrow morning? I can come in as early as you need me."

The sheriff responded: "Let's meet at seven-thirty. We'll come by Winfield's house first thing." Then he said, "I'm tired and need to get some sleep. Us old folks don't do well without sleep any better than we go up ladders. Besides," he added, "I'm not used to doing this much work on a Sunday."

The two men drove back to the county courthouse where the deputy got into his car and drove home. Kretzler was in bed, asleep, only a short time after he arrived home. He forgot to call Samuelson.

Chapter Twenty-four

Monday, September 15, 1952

The next morning, Lawrs called Pansy and asked if he had heard from either the sheriff or Samuelson. He had not. Pansy said he would call both of them.

He called Samuelson first. His secretary said he hadn't come in yet. He had an appointment outside the office and would probably be in about nine-thirty.

When he called the sheriff's office, the secretary indicated he had not come in yet. He asked if the deputy was there; she said he wasn't in, either. She indicated she would leave a message for the sheriff. Pansy told her that it was urgent.

Maybe that was a good sign. The sheriff must have caught Winfield Sunday evening and questioned him for several hours after that; that would explain why he hadn't come in early. Maybe, they were even now picking up Roy. He hoped he was right.

His instinct told him otherwise.

His instinct was correct.

The sheriff came in about eight forty-five; he returned Pansy's call. He said he and his deputy had gone over to Winfield's house last night and again this morning; they couldn't find either Winfield or Roy. Pansy asked what he would do now. The sheriff said the only thing he could think to do would be to put out a wanted bulletin for Winfield. He said he would call the state's vehicle registration bureau, get a description of Winfield's truck and it's license plate number, and call both into the highway patrol. Pansy told the sheriff Winfield drove a 1945 pickup; he made a point of telling him that it was always dirty and would look almost gray.

After he had hung up, Pansy felt miserable. He had to do something. He decided the other Rounders needed to be updated; they should get together again. He called Lawrs and told him to go to Midway by ten. He then called Mac to tell her that they were coming. She had a lot of questions for him, but he told her to wait until he got there. He asked her to call Stoner; she said she would. Finally, Pansy called Fritz.

THEY WERE ALL ASSEMBLED AT Mac's big round table just after ten o'clock. Pansy started by going over everything he knew, including things he had told some of them before. He explained what he had found out when he talked to the sheriff, and he mentioned that Samuelson was not in when he called. Finally, he reminded them that Martinek had been released.

Everyone sat for a moment, not speaking. Stoner broke the silence. "We've got to do something. Roy is in trouble. We've got to figure out where he is. Let the sheriff worry about Winfield."

"I agree," Mac said. "Where could he be? We know he's not at Winfield's house.

Lawrs had an idea. "Winfield's a postman. He'd know all the empty farmhouses on his route; maybe he stashed Roy in one of those houses. Maybe that is where he was last night when the sheriff couldn't find him."

"Good thinking, Lawrs. He could be there now," Mac added.

"Or," Lawrs said, "he might be running his regular mail route, trying not to call attention to himself or where he's keeping Roy. We should tell the sheriff to go to every house on Winfield's route."

"That's a good idea," Fritz said, "but I'm guessing it's a pretty big route. It's probably fifty farms, maybe more. I just don't know if that's practical."

Mac spoke up. "Even if it was only twenty-five places, the sheriff would have trouble finding him. He'd have to go door to door asking if Winfield had been there."

"That would take forever, and he still might not find him," Stoner said. "Why don't we help? We could be like a posse and fan out like we did on Saturday. Lawrs do you know where he delivers the mail?"

"I've got a pretty good idea. Mac, do you have a county map?"

"Yes, I'll go get it."

"Wait a minute," Fritz said. "We don't want to tackle Winfield ourselves; he's probably armed."

"Yeah, but if we see him, we could go to the nearest farmhouse and call the sheriff," Lawrs said.

"But how will we know its Winfield's truck?"

"Easy," Pansy said. "He drives a beat up 1945 Chevy pickup. It's dark green, but it's always so dirty it just looks gray. If he's parked at a farmhouse, we shouldn't have any trouble spotting him."

Fritz spoke again, "I think we ought to focus on Roy. Like Stoner said before, let the sheriff handle Winfield. We need to try to figure out where Roy is."

Again, there was a pause in the conversation as everyone thought.

Then Lawrs offered, "Let's go back to what I said before. Maybe he has him in an old abandoned house or barn along his route. That's where we should look."

"That's good, Lawrs," Mac said.

"He wouldn't leave him outdoors, and he wouldn't put him in an empty house in a town—someone could see him come and go," Fritz said. "I agree with Lawrs, he probably put him in an abandoned farmhouse."

"If that's the case," Lawrs said, "there aren't too many abandoned farms around. We ought to be able to figure out where they are. Mac, get that map."

As Mac went to get the county map, the Rounders began talking about where they knew there were abandoned farmhouses. Almost everyone at the table knew of one or two; Lawrs knew the most since he was out on rural roads more than the others were.

Mac returned with the map and spread it out on the table.

Lawrs said, "Look, I think his route covers a pretty big area, but I'm not sure exactly where it is. For safety's sake, let's assume that he gets as far north as Keystone, as far west as Lucerne, south to Blairstown, and east to Atkins." He drew a line to mark the area. Let's identify all the abandoned houses we know in the area; there might be more, but we might spot them as we drive along." Each person took turns identifying on the map where he or she knew there was an abandoned farmhouse or barn. When they got through, there were twelve places on the map with an 'x.'

"Twelve, Pansy said. "That's not too bad. We can cover them pretty quickly if we break into teams. Stoner and Mac can go together, Fritz and I can work together, and Lawrs can go alone—he's young and more energetic than the rest of us."

"Lawrs shouldn't go alone," Mac said. "This is too important. I'm just going to lock the door, put a sign on the pump that we are closed, and have Ruthie go with Lawrs. Ruthie," she said in a voice loud enough that she could be heard on the other side of the cafe, "come here. We need you." When Ruthie got there, Mac explained what was happening and told her that she would be working with Lawrs. Ruthie was ecstatic.

Fritz said, "Mac, it's great of you to let Ruthie help us, but let's rearrange the teams so that you and Stoner aren't together. You should have a man with you."

"You chauvinist," Stoner said. She was sitting beside Fritz as she usually did, and she punched him on the arm. "We're just as strong and brave as you ninnies are, but I guess it's like Dinah Shore sang awhile back, 'It's good to have a man around the house.' Rework the assignments, Pansy."

"Okay," he said. "Stoner you go with Fritz. Mac you come with me, and Ruthie can go with Lawrs. Let's make a list of the places in some logical order and give each team a few of them. We'll meet back here when we're done."

Pansy used the map to assign specific houses to each team. When he was through, he said, "It'll take Lawrs and Ruthie the longest. They've got five places, but they're close together and close to here." Each team made a rough map of the route they would take.

They agreed that they would try to be back as soon as they could. Pansy added, "If a team doesn't show up by twelve-thirty, we'll start looking for you. We'll keep this map back here so we'll know where to look." He tapped his finger on the map they had been using.

Mac told everyone that there was a key to the cafe under the mat in front of her house behind the tourist cabins. "That way, who ever gets here first can get in."

Mac and Pansy were the first ones to leave. They had the farthest distance to go, but they had only three properties to examine.

When they got to a place on their list, each team followed a similar routine: They would pull up to the abandoned house and try to get inside. They would look for signs someone had been there recently. They would also call out, hoping that if Roy were there, he would be able to answer.

If they couldn't find him in the house, they would go to whatever outbuildings there were on the farm. They were only too aware that Truesdale's uncle's body had been found in a chicken coop.

In some places, the task was easy because whoever had bought the farm had torn down the outbuildings as they began to disintegrate. In other cases, the houses themselves had been torn down, and the barn or some other building had been maintained to store grain or hay.

Once in a while, as they drove along their route, they'd see a structure standing on its own, abandoned; they stopped and examined those places.

Mac and Pansy were the first ones to return. They had an easy time. At one place on their list, the house had been torn down, and the only thing left was the barn. On another, only the house remained standing. The doors on the house were missing, so they had no trouble getting in.

The last place they investigated had a house, a barn, a machine shed, and one chicken coop. They went to the house first. The front door was locked, but Pansy went around to the back, found an unlocked window, and crawled in. Mac waited outside. After he determined there were no signs that anyone had been in the house recently, they examined each of the outbuildings. They found nothing.

When Pansy and Mac got back to Midway, each had a cup of coffee. Pansy was hungry, so Mac made him a sandwich. The 'closed' sign was still up on the door, and the front window shades of the cafe were pulled down.

Fritz and Stoner were back next. They had three houses on their list and had been successful in getting into each one. Only two of the properties had outbuildings, and they were able to walk through them quickly. At one house, the doors were all boarded up, and they saw no reason to suggest any of the boards had been pulled down recently. Along their route, they spotted a fourth property and examined it. It consisted only of an abandoned house and a barn.

Fritz and Stoner both had a sandwich while the four Rounders waited for Ruthie and Lawrs to return.

Twelve o'clock came and went. Twelve-fifteen passed. By twelve-thirty, they were really worried.

By twelve forty-five, Ruthie and Lawrs still hadn't returned. The other Rounders decided to set out to trace their route.

Chapter Twenty-five

Monday, September 15, 1952

Ruthie and Lawrs started out from Midway in his pickup. It took them fifteen minutes to get to the first place on their list. It was small—four rooms downstairs and a single bedroom upstairs. The front door of the house was missing, so it was easy to enter. As they walked through the rooms, they found no footprints or anything else that indicated Roy had been there.

Outside, there was a machine shed, an outhouse, and a corncrib. Only the corncrib had been maintained; it was still being used it to store grain. They found no helpful clues in any of the buildings.

"This is really spooky, isn't it?" Ruthie said as they walked back to Lawrs' pickup. "I feel sorry for the family that used to live here. It's small, but they must have loved it—raising their kids here and everything."

"Sure," Lawrs said, somewhat cynically, "but remember, they were poor enough that they had to sell the farm."

"How do you know that?"

"This is a small farm, and it's harder to keep them going."

"Why? I would think it would be easier."

"The basic equipment you need to run a farm is expensive; if you don't have enough land, you can't afford to pay for it."

"So what happens to small farms?"

"A farmer buys them to increase the size of his own place, and with more land, he can afford more efficient equipment. For example, right now everybody is shifting to four-row corn pickers because you can harvest corn faster; they're expensive."

"Oh," she said, pausing to think. "That makes it even sadder."

The second farm had a house, a garage, and machine shed. The barn had burned down, its charred timbers on the ground. Lawrs speculated that it had probably been struck by lightening, and there had been no one around to put the fire out. After fifteen minutes of looking, they could find no signs of Roy and went on to the third house.

It was a one-story, square building. The roof pitched up to a single point from the four exterior walls. There was a small porch on the right front of the house.

As they approached the house, they could see that the weeds in the gravel drive had been run over; there were recent tire tracks.

They went up onto the porch. The front door was closed, but not locked. Lawrs cautiously opened the door.

In the first room, the only light was coming from the door that they entered and one window. It had been boarded over, but most of the boards had fallen off. As they entered the room, they could also see footprints in the dust.

Lawrs called out, "Roy, are you here? It's Lawrs and Ruthie."

Instantly they heard Roy answer. "Lawrs? Is that you?"

The voice was coming from the next room. They rushed to the door and opened it. Roy was lying on the cot, his hands and feet tied. He was still in his nightclothes.

"Oh, God!" Roy said. "It's you. I've never been happier to see two people in my entire life."

"I'll untie you," Lawrs said. He usually carried a small pocketknife, but he didn't have it today. He started the slower process of manually untying the knots. First, he was able to release Roy's hands. He then worked on the rope around his legs.

As Lawrs was working to loosen the knots, Ruthie asked, "Roy, how long have you been here?"

"He brought me here Friday. I didn't see him again until Saturday. He told me that I was unconscious most of the time. On Saturday, he brought me some water and food. He did the same on Sunday."

"Have you been tied up all this time?"

"He'd untie my hands so I could eat. Then he'd retie them and untie my feet so I could walk around a bit. He hasn't been here today."

"Oh, you poor man. I'm so sorry," Ruthie said.

Lawrs was finally able to untie his legs and tried to help Roy stand, but he couldn't stand on his own. He fell back to a sitting position on the edge of the cot. "Let me sit here a minute." He swung his legs back and forth and continued to rub his hands to get the blood circulating.

"Who did this?" Lawrs asked. "We guessed it might be Sam Winfield. We found you by looking for abandoned houses on his mail route, " Lawrs said.

Roy answered him. "Yes, it was Winfield. I discovered something he didn't want anyone to know. At first, he wore a mask and altered his voice. Later, he didn't hide his identity. I got a lot out of him about why he did what he did."

Roy started to explain when Winfield suddenly rushed through the door from the adjacent room.

He had seen Lawrs' truck, stopped his own truck on the road, and walked to the house. The front door was open, so he had no trouble getting in without making a noise. He did not have his hood on, but he was holding a shotgun in his hand.

"What the hell are you two doing here?" he said, pointing the gun at all three people in the room.

"We might ask you the same question, Winfield," Ruthie said boldly. "Why have you got Roy tied up? Why did you hit him? Just look at the bruise on his head and the blood on his clothes!" Ruthie was shouting. Lawrs was amazed at her assertiveness.

"Shut up," Winfield said. "How did you find this place?"

Lawrs responded, "We're not stupid, you know; we figured out it was you and guessed you'd have him in some old house on your mail route."

"Who else knows?" Winfield asked.

"Everybody," Lawrs said, stretching the truth. "The sheriff, Everett Samuelson, and all the other Rounders. They'll be here in minutes. We've all been searching. We just happened to be the ones that got to him first. The others are on their way."

"I don't believe you," Winfield said. "Do you think I am stupid?"

"It's true. We have three teams looking for Roy. We divided up your mail route, and this house was on our list. They agreed if we weren't back at Midway by noon, they would start looking for us."

Looking at her watch for effect, Ruthie said, "They would have started looking for us three-quarters of an hour ago. They know the route we took. You can't get away."

As she spoke, Roy stood up; he was still weak. He slumped against Lawrs, who held him firmly.

"Just give me your gun, Mr. Winfield," Ruthie said. "Don't make things worse than they are. If you do, they'll go easy on you." It sounded like a line she had heard on a radio crime drama. Lawrs was impressed; how bold she was.

"Be quiet, girl!" he said. "I should shoot you all. Right here. Now!"

"If you do, they'll know who did it, and they'll be right on your trail. There's no place you can hide," Ruthie responded firmly.

Winfield didn't know what to do. It was a lose-lose situation. If what they said was true, and he killed them, the sheriff would know he did it. If he let them go, they would be after him just as fast. "How did you know it was me?" he asked.

Lawrs spoke up, "Roy figured out you were Truesdale's half-brother, didn't you, Roy?"

Roy didn't speak. He just nodded his head.

"That meant you were the one who killed Truesdale and his uncle—your uncle," he said with emphasis.

"I did not kill my uncle. Truesdale did that."

"Now who's stupid?" Ruthie asked. "Why would he do that?"

"Our mother left her money to both of us. Because I'd been adopted, she didn't know where I was. She asked Truesdale to find me and give me my share. He wouldn't. She asked her brother for help. He and Truesdale had a fight about it. That's when Truesdale shot him. When I came to Truesdale's later, he bragged about what he'd done. He was going to shoot me, but I wrestled his gun away and shot him."

"If that's the case," Lawrs said, "they'll go easy on you. You did it in self-defense, right? You were just trying to protect yourself. They probably will let you off." He didn't believe what he was saying, but he hoped it would get Winfield to back off.

Speaking to Lawrs, Winfield said, "Get on the floor." Then he waved his gun at Ruthie and said, "Tie them both up. There's more rope in that corner." Neither Lawrs nor Ruthie moved; by this time Roy was sitting on the cot again. "You heard me, Lawrs, get on the floor. And you," addressing Ruthie again, "tie them both up." —Apparently, he didn't know Ruthie's name or couldn't remember it.

Lawrs, reluctantly, got down on the floor.

"Just let us go," Roy said weakly. "You can get a head start if you go now."

"No, you damned fool. Tie them up, girl. Now!" He pointed at

Lawrs with his gun and said, "Lie down flat on your stomach and put your hands behind your back."

Ruthie started to tie Lawrs, making the cords as loose as she could.

"Tighter," Winfield yelled. She did as he told her.

When she finished tying up Lawrs, he was on the floor, one side of his face in the dust. Winfield pointed at Roy, "Now, tie him up, again—the way you found him."

Roy was about to collapse. He moaned and said softly, "No, please, no." He looked into Ruthie's eyes, hoping she could save him from being tied to the cot again. She looked away and picked up the ropes.

"Sam, don't do this. Let us go. We promise not to tell them that you were here," Lawrs said desperately, looking up from the floor, one side of his face dirty.

"I don't trust you," Sam said meanly.

He pointed the shotgun toward Ruthie and Roy. "Tie him up," he shouted. She stalled as long as she could stall, hoping that the Rounders would show up. He shouted at her again, so she finished tying Roy to the cot.

"Now, girl, you're coming with me," he said, moving toward her and roughly putting his arm around her throat as he continued to hold the gun. "You're going to insure that I get out of here safely."

Chapter Twenty-six

Monday, September 15, 1952

The four people sitting at Midway were extremely upset. Ruthie and Lawrs should have been back some time ago. They had to act. They looked at the map and prepared to follow the route the young pair had taken.

Fritz said, "We have to call the sheriff. This is dangerous. Let's have him start with the same list of places, but start from the end of the route that's closest to Vinton. We'll start at the place closest to here. By the time we meet in the middle, either we will have found them, or the sheriff will." Everyone agreed.

Fritz called the sheriff. He was in and clearly had done nothing except call around to other police stations, sheriffs' offices, and the highway patrol. It wasn't as though he wasn't concerned; he was, but he didn't know what to do next. He had talked with Samuelson, and he was at a loss, too.

Fritz explained to the sheriff what they had been doing and what they needed him to do. He told him to find a county map; he would help him identify the five places that Ruthie and Lawrs were supposed to inspect in their effort to find Roy.

The sheriff stood in front of the county map on his wall while

Fritz talked him through the route he should take. The first place he identified for the sheriff was the last house on the Rounders' list; it was closest to Vinton, the furthest point from Midway. He worked through the other four places on the list, identifying the houses in the reverse order that Lawrs and Ruthie were supposed to inspect them. When they had finished, the group prepared to leave.

Fritz asked if anyone had a gun. Pansy had a rifle across the back of his pickup window, and Stoner said she had a pistol under the front seat of her car. "Let's take two vehicles," Pansy said. "We will at least have some back up that way."

They split up. Fritz and Stoner were in Stoner's car with Stoner's handgun, and Pansy and Mac were in his pickup with the rifle that had been hanging across the back window now in Mac's hand. "There's nothing funny about it, Pansy, but I feel as though I'm riding shotgun on a stagecoach with Johnny Mack Brown or somebody," Mac said, with the butt of the gun on the car's floor.

"Do you think I look like Johnny Mack Brown?" Pansy asked.

"No, more like Roy Rogers." She was trying to lighten the mood.

"Does that make you Dale Evans?"

"I guess, but I doubt if she ever road shotgun."

The humor came hard, but it helped relieve the stress of wondering what had happened to their friends.

The Rounders got to the first place on Ruthie and Lawrs' list in the same time it had taken the younger couple to get there—about fifteen minutes. Fritz and Stoner looked through the house while Pansy and Mac examined the outbuildings. Both teams saw footprints in the dust that had settled on the floors of all the buildings. They concluded that they belonged to their two friends because one set was large and the other small, suggesting the presence of a man and a woman. There was no third set of prints.

It took the sheriff a bit longer to get to the first house on his list, the first one of the five coming from the north. He and his deputy found the place boarded up. The house didn't seem to have been disturbed at all—no evidence that anyone had been there. The same held true for the garage and the barn. There were some hog houses out back and an old root cellar. They found nothing suspicious.

Their second location was even more abandoned; the house was no longer standing. All that remained was a barn that was still being used for the storage of hay, and a round, metal corn bin that probably would be full of corn in a few weeks; it was empty now. The sheriff told his deputy to get down on his knees and stick his head through the small opening at the bottom of the bin. He did as he was told. "Nothing," he reported.

The barn took a little longer to inspect. Remembering the sheriff's remarks about not doing ladders well, Mosley said he would go up to the hayloft while the sheriff examined the ground floor. Neither of them saw any signs that anyone had been there recently.

The second place the Rounders visited had only a few buildings. Divided into pairs, they quickly were able to inspect them all. Again, there were footprints to indicate Ruthie and Lawrs had been there, but no third person.

As they approached the third house from the south, they could see that it had been abandoned, but they could also see a truck parked along the road. Pansy could tell it was the pickup Winfield used for mail delivery; it looked empty. Lawrs' pickup was there too, but it was in the yard, closer to the house.

Pansy and Mac were in the lead. As soon as Pansy saw the two vehicles, he motioned out the window with his left hand for Fritz and Stoner to keep following him as they all passed by the house. He was afraid that if either car stopped in front of the house or pulled into the yard, Winfield would be alerted, and he might do something drastic. Fortunately, just beyond a cornfield on the north side of the house, the road curved to the right and there was a small grove of cottonwood trees where both vehicles could park without being seen.

On any other day, this would have been an idyllic scene: a small stream, the old cottonwoods, their leaves a golden yellow; there was a pleasant breeze. You could even smell burning leaves from some distant farm.

All four people got out of their vehicles and stood talking. "Here's what we should do," Pansy said. "Fritz and I will walk back to the house as quietly as we can. Stoner, give Fritz your pistol; Mac, I'll take my rifle."

Speaking to Mac and Stoner, "You two wait here beside the road for the sheriff; he's got to be along soon. When he comes, tell him where we are, and let him figure out what to do."

"Meanwhile," he continued, "Fritz and I will go through the corn field and try to surprise Winfield in the house. We'll try to calm him down. Everyone okay with that?" They all nodded.

Pansy and Fritz started walking south. They entered the cornfield that stood between the place where they had parked their two vehicles and the house. Stoner and Mac went out to the road and waited; they couldn't be seen because of the trees and the turn in the road.

Pansy and Fritz couldn't be seen as the approached from the north: the cornfield shielded them, and the house had no windows on the north in order to protect it from winter winds. As they crept along the cornrows, Pansy sad, "Thank God they haven't picked the corn."

When they got to the edge of the cornfield closest to the house, Fritz asked, "Should we split up? I'll take the back, and you take the front."

Pansy thought for a few seconds. "No, let's stick together. The front door's open. We don't know about the back one; it could be locked."

Fritz guessed at the layout of the house, "There are probably four rooms. The porch goes into the front room. If they're not there, you go straight back, and I'll go left into the other room on the front. Whoever finds them first should circle right, and the other guy circle left when he gets there. That way we can surround him."

"Good idea," Pansy said.

There was silence for a few seconds.

"Well," Pansy said, "no time like the present. Let's go." He started to run; Fritz was beside him. The lawn between the edge of the cornfield and the north side of the house was only about four or five yards wide. They were up to the stoop in five strides. It was two more strides across the porch to the front room. As they entered, they could see the room was empty. Pansy went straight ahead through the open door to the next room; Fritz went left to the side room.

Winfield had just put his arm around Ruthie's throat as Pansy ran into the room, moved to the right, and held his gun on Winfield. Winfield turned to face Pansy; he still had his arm around Ruthie's throat. Before anyone could speak, Fritz rushed into the room to the left, behind Winfield.

"You're covered, Winfield; put the gun down," Pansy said.

Winfield knew Fritz was behind him, but facing Pansy, he said. "You sons-a-bitches. If you shoot me, she gets it." However, he wasn't positioned to shoot Ruthie without shooting himself since he had one arm around her neck and held the shotgun with the other hand. Recognizing the situation, he pushed Ruthie to the floor, freeing his other arm to point the gun toward her. As she fell, he said, "I swear I'll shoot her. You may get me, but I'll get her."

Pansy, speaking softly and calmly, repeated his words. "Winfield, just put the gun down."

Ruthie spoke up from the floor, "He says he didn't kill Truesdale's uncle, and he killed Truesdale only when he attacked him. Tell him that they'll let him off for self-defense."

"If that's true, they'll go lightly," Fritz said, still standing behind Winfield. He continued to point Stoner's revolver at him, but as he looked over the top of the gun, he could see there were no bullets in the chambers. He didn't let on and continued to point the gun at Winfield, hoping he would not turn around and notice.

The three men held their positions for what seemed an interminably long time.

Suddenly, the sheriff appeared at the door, pointing his gun at Winfield. "Put the gun down, Winfield, I've got you now."

It was all too much for Winfield; he wasn't a killer. He'd gotten himself into a mess, and he didn't know how to get out of it. He slowly bent over and put the shotgun on the floor, putting his hands up as he straightened out.

"Get his gun, Walt," the sheriff said forcefully.

As Walt reached for the gun on the floor, the sheriff said, "You're under arrest for the murder of John Truesdale and his uncle. Cuff him, Walt."

By this time, Stoner and Mac were in the room.

They had been standing beside the road only a few minutes when the sheriff showed up. They hailed him, and through his car's open window, they quickly told him what was happening. Without waiting, he had driven off with his deputy toward the house. They had parked behind Lawrs' car, quietly closing their doors so that they wouldn't alert Winfield. Stoner and Mac followed the sheriff's car, half walking, half running along the road to the house. At one point, Stoner had twisted her ankle in the loose gravel, but she kept on running.

As she entered, Stoner saw Fritz and ran to him. "Fritz, thank God you're safe. I was so worried." She pulled his head down toward her and kissed him on the cheek. You old devil," she said.

Meanwhile, Mac ran to Roy's side and kneeled beside the cot. "Roy, let me help untie you, you poor man. What has he done to you? You're all bloody."

"Hey, somebody untie me," Lawrs called out. Ruthie was getting up from the floor when he called, and she instantly ran to him, dropping to her knees to loosen the ropes she had only just tied.

No one noticed as the sheriff and his deputy started to lead Winfield out of the room. As he reached the door, he turned to the Rounders and said, "All I can say is that you are all damned fools. You should have let me taken care of this!"

Pansy thought to himself: if we had, old man, more than one of us would be dead, and you'd still be sitting in your office. But he said nothing, just thankful to have the ordeal over.

By this time, Mac had Roy's ropes off and tried to help him stand. He was too weak; he fell back into a sitting position on the cot. Mac leaned over and gave him a kiss on the forehead. "You old coot; you really had us all worried. At least you're okay now." Pansy came over to help him up.

"Let's all get the hell out of here," Pansy said, "Roy, I'll take you home. We'll go see Doc Newland first. Stay here and I'll get my truck. It'll take me a couple of minutes. Lawrs, can you take Ruthie and Mac back to Midway?"

"Sure," Lawrs said. "The cab will easily hold three people."

"I'll be glad to sit in the middle," Ruthie said.

Pansy then said to Stoner, "Stoner, can you take Fritz home in your car?"

"Sure," she said.

Stoner looked at Fritz and asked, "Go get the car and bring it over here. I don't want to walk back. I twisted my ankle on that gravel when I ran over here."

"You bet," Fritz said. He held Stoner's revolver out to her. "Here's your gun. After we got in here, I realized it wasn't loaded. Next time, bring some bullets along with you." He smiled.

Stoner said, "Oh, dear, I thought it was loaded."

As they all moved out of the room where Roy and the others had been held, Mac saw three boxes on the floor in the front room; they were open. One was Dot's antique walnut box. The second contained her silver. In the third, she saw her Native American artifacts. She came to a complete stop and looked at them. Then she began to cry softly.

Lawrs came up and put his arm around Mac; he didn't see the boxes at first. "What's wrong Mac? Everyone one is safe now."

She pointed to the boxes, her voice breaking up, "There, look, my artifacts," she said. She could say no more.

Everyone in the room gathered around the boxes, staring at the contents, and looking at Mac. There wasn't a dry eye in the room. The only one who wasn't fully aware of what was going on was Roy. He remained in a partial state of shock. Pansy was still supporting him.

"Oh, my," she said. "I thought they were gone forever." She leaned over and started to lift some of the items up.

"Pansy, help me," Lawrs said, "we'll put the boxes in the back of my pickup." He picked up the heaviest box, the one with the silver in it, and Pansy picked up the walnut box. Mac picked up the box with the artifacts and followed them to the truck. Stoner supported Roy. They would have to wait until Pansy and Fritz brought the vehicles to the house.

The sheriff and his deputy had already taken Winfield out to their car and put him in the back seat. The sheriff turned around to the others as they came out of the house. "We'll get this son-of-a-bitch back to Vinton and lock him up. I'll come back to get his truck later. You all go home where you belong and forget about this. It's all over. I've got my criminal."

Stoner said softly in response to the sheriff's statement, "It will only be over, old man, when we can put this behind us, and that will be awhile." The sheriff didn't hear, but everyone else did.

Ruthie said to Lawrs as she and Mac got inside his truck, "Oh, you were so brave, Lawrs."

He certainly didn't feel as though he was the brave one of the pair. "No, you were the brave one, Ruthie. I was really impressed." He looked directly into her eyes and gave her a small kiss on one cheek.

Chapter Twenty-seven

Thursday, September 18, 1952

Pansy called Everett Samuelson and asked him if he would attend the next Thursday morning meeting of the Rounders. He knew Everett would know better than anyone what was happening at the courthouse in Vinton.

When the Rounders were all assembled, Mac called to Ruthie, "Beers all around, my dear; we all need one, and take one for yourself. If I had Champagne, we'd break it out." Mac had locked up the cafe as she had when they went they all went looking for Roy.

Most of the Rounders didn't drink that early—but Pansy took a Hamm's as soon as it was offered.

Lawrs hesitated, and then took one. Ruthie looked into his eyes as she handed it to him and said softly, "Thank heavens you're okay, Lawrs." He looked directly into her eyes, smiled, and thanked her.

Mac took a beer as well, but she didn't drink it; it just stood open in front of her for the rest of the morning. Everyone else chose coffee except Roy; he asked for hot tea.

When Ruthie had finished serving everyone, Mac told her to sit down, pointing to an empty chair she had placed next to Lawrs. Ruthie couldn't have been happier.

Pansy started the discussion by asking Samuelson, "What have they done with Winfield?"

Samuelson had everyone's full attention. "He's been arraigned for manslaughter for killing Truesdale. He's also been indicted for kidnapping Roy and threatening Ruthie and Lawrs with a lethal weapon."

Pansy almost shouted, "Manslaughter! Why not murder?"

"What about the uncle?" Stoner butted in. "Isn't he being charged with that?"

"They have decided not to charge him with the death of his uncle," Samuelson said. "They're inclined to believe Winfield's story that Truesdale killed him. It's manslaughter for killing Truesdale not first-degree murder because the prosecutor believes it wasn't premeditated."

"Hog wash," Stoner said. "Why would Winfield have gone to Truesdale's farm except to kill him?"

Samuelson clarified in his usual, methodical way: "What he told the sheriff was that he went to Truesdale's three times. First, to tell Truesdale he had discovered they were half-brothers. Later, the uncle arrived, and Truesdale told him about Winfield's identity. The uncle said he wanted to meet him. When Winfield came back the second time, the uncle told them that their mother wanted them to split her money evenly. Truesdale refused because he needed the money to pay his debts—as Roy discovered at the courthouse. Winfield left after a shouting match."

Samuelson continued, "After a few days, Winfield came back a third time to talk about the money; he wanted his share. When he got there, Truesdale refused to give him any. He bragged that he had shot their uncle when they got into a fight over the money. He said he'd used his uncle's own revolver to kill him. It was at this third meeting that Truesdale and Winfield got into a fight, and Truesdale threatened Winfield with his shotgun. During the fight,

Winfield got the gun away from Truesdale and shot him. That's why they haven't charged Winfield with first-degree murder; assuming his story is correct, it was not pre-meditated. To be pre-meditated, he would have brought a gun with him—but he didn't. He killed Truesdale with his own shotgun. They believe it was Truesdale's gun because they found loaded shells in a bureau in his bedroom with his prints on them. After the fight, Winfield took the shotgun home. He bought some shells for it, and that's the gun he used when he kidnapped Roy and held Lawrs and Ruthie."

Lawrs asked, "Roy, would you go over how you knew Winfield was Truesdale's half-brother."

Roy took his time to explain, "It's complicated. Several months ago he told me that the Winfields had told him that they had adopted him, but they didn't know who his birth parents were. After the Winfields died, he wanted to find them. I told him that he would have to petition the district court to open the adoption records. I prepared the papers, he signed them, and I delivered them."

He continued, "We didn't hear from the court for quite a while, so after one our Rounders' meetings he attended here at Midway, I privately told him that I'd go over and try to push the judge to act. He told me not to bother. He said a cousin—one he didn't even know he had—had contacted him. She told him the name of his mother."

"How did she know?" Stoner asked.

"Before she died, the cousin's grandmother had told the cousin that her granddaughter, Winfield's mother, had a child out of wedlock and had put it up for adoption. The grandmother knew who had adopted the child."

"But how could she have known who adopted him and the mother didn't?"

"The cousin told Winfield that it was his grandmother who had arranged for the adoption, not his mother; she didn't want to know who had adopted him. Remember, when he told me all of this, he did not tell me his mother's name."

Addressing Mac, Roy continued, "He took the antique box you bought from Dot because, in addition to the county history, the old Bible contained genealogical charts. They both had information about the early Caldwells."

"But when we were all at the table and he went over to look for the name Caldwell, he told us that there weren't any Caldwell entries in the county history," Mac said.

"Technically, he was right. There weren't any main entries for a Caldwell in the county history. But there were references to Caldwells in the detailed index in back. He discovered them, along with the genealogical charts at the back of the Bible, when he went over to look at the box the second time, when the meeting was over. Remember, Fritz, you and he spent some time going through things in the box."

"Yes, I remember," Fritz said.

"When he saw Caldwell references in the county history and Caldwell entries in the genealogical charts in the back of the Bible, he was afraid they would reveal his identity and his tie to Truesdale. By that time, he had killed Truesdale and he didn't want people to make the connection. He also wanted some of the family photos in the box because he thought they included some of his older relatives. He had started the whole process to get a sense of connection to his past family history, and some of the records in the box helped him make that connection. To cover his tracks, he took your artifacts and sterling silver, Mac."

"He wasn't interested in my Meskawaki artifacts or the silver?" Mac asked.

"No, he just took them to cover up what he really wanted."

"Oh, my heavens," Mac exclaimed.

"But how did the stuff from his family get into the box and why was it at Dot's?" Ruthie asked."

Stoner answered, "I told the others, Ruthie, but you probably didn't hear: Dot said she bought the box at an estate sale back in Ohio while she was visiting her sister in Marietta. That's where the Truesdales and the Caldwells lived in the early 1800s. Lots of people in that area later moved to Iowa. Mac saw the name Truesdale in the county history in the box; that's why she bought it."

Roy continued, "When he first told me that he'd found his birth mother, I didn't ask her name. I didn't find that out until the court mailed me the adoption papers. I got them because I was his lawyer. The fact that I got them at all was almost an accident. After he told me that story about his cousin finding him, I tried to go to the county judge's clerk twice to explain we didn't need to have the records opened. But I never did. The first time, I forgot. The second time, I remembered, but I had to run to catch the bus home."

"When did you get them?" Mac asked.

"I got them after the last Rounders' meeting—the day before he kidnapped me. When I realized his mother's name was Caldwell, I figured out what it meant. I called Winfield and asked him if he knew he was Truesdale's half-brother. When he discovered I knew, I guess he felt he needed to silence me because he thought I would tell people, and they would figure out his connection to Truesdale's death."

"That fits," Fritz said. "When we were looking for you, Roy, I asked the Belle Plaine telephone switchboard operator if she had placed a call for to you; she told me about the call you made to Robinson. She said there was a second call, but she couldn't remember the name of the person you called. It must have been your call to Winfield."

"Why did Truesdale put his uncle in the chicken coop and put the car in the ravine?" Lawrs asked.

"He panicked; he didn't know what to do. He hid the body in the chicken coop and chained the dog outside to keep people away. He put the revolver in the truck and drove it into the ravine. He planned to go back and get rid of everything, but he didn't have time—or at least that's what he told Truesdale during their argument."

"Gosh," Lawrs said. "That's almost exactly what I said he did, isn't it Pansy?"

"Yeah, you're one bright kid," Pansy said. "Now, if you were only as bright about some of the other things you do." He smiled. Lawrs understood what he was saying. Ruthie didn't.

"So, who was having the argument that Jim Ross overheard?" Lawrs asked.

"We don't know for sure," Samuelson said. "Truesdale argued with four people before he was killed: Robinson, Martinek, his uncle, and, of course, Winfield. Take your pick."

"God," Stoner said, "the man fought with everyone."

"So, Robinson had nothing to do with all of this?" Lawrs asked. "For a while, I really thought he killed Truesdale."

Samuelson just shook his head.

"Roy, do you think he would have killed you?" Mac asked.

"I don't know," Roy said slowly. "I think he didn't know what he would do with me. After he revealed himself to me at the old house, we talked a lot. He wasn't mad at me personally; he was just afraid and didn't know what to do. But he felt he couldn't let me go."

"You poor guy," she said.

"Did Winfield came to our Rounders' meeting to get us off the scent?" Stoner asked.

"Yes," Roy said. "The first time he sat in was an accident; we just happened to be talking about Truesdale's murder when he came to deliver the mail. He wanted to know how much we were going to find out, so he came to more meetings. At the last one, when we talked about Martinek, you'll remember he tried to reinforce our belief that he did it."

"We haven't talked about Martinek," Mac said. "They let him go without charging him with anything?"

"Yes and no," Samuelson said. "They have charged him with threatening the sheriff and resisting arrest, but not murder. They released him on bail just before Winfield attacked Roy. When Winfield found out that Martinek was out, and Roy knew he was Truesdale's brother, he decided it was time to act against Roy. He thought Martinek's release would put the police off his own trail."

Lawrs asked, "But how do they know that Winfield didn't shoot his uncle? Everything you've told us came from Winfield, right? He could have lied so that he'd only be charged with manslaughter or self-defense for killing Truesdale. If he killed the uncle, he wouldn't have gotten off so easily."

Again, Samuelson had an answer. "The revolver Lawrs found in the truck only had Truesdale's finger prints on it; Winfield's prints weren't on it. And the state ballistic experts determined that a bullet they shot from that gun matched the bullet that killed the uncle."

"Boy, that was pretty stupid," Pansy said, "leaving fingerprints on the gun."

"Truesdale wiped most of the fingerprints off," Samuelson said, "but he forgot that when you load a revolver, versus a pistol, a portion of the cylinder you touch when you load it stops behind the gun's barrel as you twist it around. He didn't think to turn the cylinder to wipe off that fingerprint. He also made the mistake of not understanding, I guess, or he just forgot, that the cartridges themselves had his finger prints on them."

"Boy, he was really dumb about guns," Pansy said.

Lawrs confessed, "I'm not sure that I would have thought about the revolver business."

"Well, all you think about is girls anyway," Stoner said with a smile. "We wouldn't expect you to be an expert on guns, at least not that kind." Except for Ruthie, everyone else laughed; they understood exactly what she was saying.

"What about Dot's?" Stoner asked. "Did Truesdale's uncle rob her place?"

"No. That was done by someone else for reasons that had nothing to do with the rest of the mess," Samuelson said.

"This is all too much to take in," Mac said. "I never realized how it all connected or the risks we were taking."

"The sheriff agrees with you," Samuelson said. "He called to tell me to scold all of you for going after Roy. He claimed he could have handled it all himself. He said he knew it was Winfield, and he had a plan for finding him and Roy."

"That's hog wash," Stoner said. "He knew nothing about Winfield; he just wants to take all the credit for himself."

"I guess you could say that," Samuelson said with a slight grin on his face. "Remember, he has to stand for re-election in a couple of years."

"At least he was pretty gutsy in capturing Martinek," Stoner said. "And, he tried to capture Winfield."

"What kind of sentence will Winfield get?" Pansy asked Samuelson.

"Well his lawyer might get him off—at least on the manslaughter charge; he'll probably be able to make a pretty good case for self-defense. He will get some time for abducting Roy and threatening Lawrs and Ruthie."

"What do you mean, his lawyer? You're his lawyer aren't you?"

"No, I had to withdraw from the case. The judge felt I had a conflict of interest because of my close relationship with Roy—sorry old man. He appointed Seth Thompson as his lawyer."

"Well," Roy said, "I'm glad you aren't his lawyer; you'd get him off. Thompson might not be so successful; he's not as bright or as experienced as you are."

"Amen," Stoner said. "Let's hear it for incompetent lawyers! Winfield needs to sit in prison for a good long time after what he put us all through."

She continued, "What do we know about Shelia?"

"She has admitted to the sheriff that she didn't think Truesdale was the father," Samuelson said. "She has narrowed it down to two men, but she can't prove it was either one of them."

"I figured you were the dad, Lawrs! How did you get off so easy?" Pansy asked.

"Oh come on, Pansy. You know me better than that!" Lawrs was not smiling for once.

Ruthie, who was still sitting beside him, said, "You better not be the dad, Lawrs." She swatted him on the head with a paper napkin she had been holding.

Mac and most of the others smiled but didn't say anything.

Pansy, shifting the focus, said, "You will all be surprised to know that Martinek was by my place yesterday. He was actually speaking to me. I told him that I was sorry to have called the sheriff, but he said he understood. He didn't exactly apologize, but he did say that his temper got the best of him. He also said he was going to help support his grandchild."

"Maybe he'll become a human yet," Stoner said, somewhat skeptically. "The proof of the pudding will be when he comes to the co-op next month with his truck full of corn."

"Well, we're through with all of this," Roy said. "As much as I enjoy our meetings, maybe this should be our last one. See the mess we got ourselves in? See the mess you got me in? We should have stayed out of it."

"Oh, come on, Roy, you loved the mess—except the part where you got kidnapped," Lawrs said with a big smile on his face. "And besides, if we don't continue meeting, who am I going to tell my farmer jokes to? Speaking of which—"

"Oh, no, not that," Mac said. "Surely you are not going to tell us another farmer joke!"

"Is Homer in it?" Pansy said pseudo-seriously.

"As a matter of fact he is," He then told his story, adjusting it to the circumstances of what they had just gone through. "These two country boys, half-brothers, sons of Homer, were fooling around one day and thought it would be a good prank to push over the outhouse on their dad's farm. They crept up like a couple of commandos, pushed the outhouse over, and headed for the woods. They circled around and returned home from a different direction, so no one would suspect they had done it. When they got home, Homer approached them with a switch in his hand and yelled, 'Did you two push the outhouse over this afternoon?' The older son replied, 'We learned in school that George Washington never told a lie. Yes, Father, we pushed over the outhouse.' As a result, Homer used the switch on the boys and sent them to bed without supper. In the morning, the two half-brothers meekly approached the breakfast table and took their seats. Everything was quiet until Homer said, 'Have you two learned your lesson?' 'Sure, Dad!' said the big brother, 'But in school we learned that when George Washington told his father that he'd chopped down the cherry tree, his father forgave him because he told the truth.' 'Ah, yes!' Homer said. 'But George's dad wasn't sitting in the cherry tree when he chopped it down!'" Everyone laughed.

Just before they were all about to leave, Mac announced, "Listen everyone; lunch is on me." She said to Ruthie, who was still sitting beside Lawrs, "Ruthie, loose meat sandwiches all around and another beer for everyone."

Ruthie was crushed. Her chance to talk to Lawrs alone was gone.

Then Mac added, "And, Ruthie, fix one for yourself and come back and eat with us. You can sit next to Lawrs."

Read on for an excerpt from the second

Rounders Mystery:

Murder in Three Acts

Go to The Rounders website to get details on when it will be published and how you can get it:

www.Roundersmysteries.com

or

www.CLHutchins.com

On the website you will find information about the author, descriptions of the Rounders characters, upcoming books, the author's blog, pictures from the 1950s, fifties trivia, and jokes.

Preview

Murder In Three Acts

A Rounders Mystery

It was November 11, 1953, the thirty-fifth anniversary of the Armistice that ended World War I. Willard Carlisle always approached the anniversary with trepidation. In 1918 he had been an officer in France when the Armistice was signed. It was a great day for the Western Allies, a day of incredible celebration. But on each anniversary of the day, Willard couldn't help thinking about all the soldiers he had commanded who had died as the result of the German Kaiser's insane ambition. Such a waste of human life. It was even more depressing when he thought about what he had seen during the two years following the Armistice when he had been stationed in war-ravaged Germany. What had happened to the Allies had been bad enough, but what had happened to the German people had been an even greater catastrophe.

That evening, with Armistice Day still very much on his mind, he attended the first of two dress rehearsals for the play, *Our Town*. Charlene, his young, second wife, was playing Emily, the female lead in the play. Other members of the cast included three of six Rounders, all friends who meet at a roadside cafe called Midway once a week for coffee and conversation. Those cast in the play were: Mildred Stone (Stoner), Lawrence Jensen (Lawrs), and Fritz McKay. Ruthie Williamson, the waitress at Midway, also had a small part.

Willard had paid for the renovation of the King Theater in Belle Plaine as an inducement to get Charlene to leave New York when he retired from the Wall Street brokerage firm he had founded after the war. He had also promised her that she could build the house of her dreams on a rural estate south of town. Whatever she wanted, he had said—if she would just move to Belle Plaine with him. He had plenty of money.

Charlene was a voluptuous, natural blonde. Her great ambition had been to be a Broadway star, but she had never been able to get even a small role, in part, because she still retained some of her Bronx accent.

She was in charge of the project of turning the old movie theater into a legitimate theater and starting a community theater company; she saw this as a chance to finally realize her ambition. She believed that when people saw what she could do, they would recognize her talent, and she would be able to get parts in Chicago and, eventually, on Broadway.

Willard had moved back to his hometown to retire; he wanted to escape the stress of Wall Street and the frenetic pace of living in New York. He had also looked forward to strengthening his lifelong friendship with Fritz McKay. They had attended high school and college together, parting ways when Willard became a commissioned officer, and Fritz enlisted in World War I. They had continued to visit each other throughout the years although Fritz had traveled to New York more often than Willard came to Belle Plaine.

Willard and Charlene had driven separately to the theatre that evening, anticipating that Charlene would stay after the rehearsal to talk with the director and the cast. When she had come down into the auditorium where he had been sitting after the rehearsal had ended, she had kissed him and told him she would be home by 11:30.

By 12:15 he began to worry. When she still wasn't home by 12:45, he drove the short distance to town. When he got to there, her new Cadillac convertible was still parked outside the theatre. He went to the doors; they were locked and the lobby was dark.

He drove a few blocks to the home of the theater's director, Malcolm Walters. Charlene had first met Walters when she had moved to Chicago for two years, hoping to start an acting career there. When that had not worked out, she had moved back to New York where she met Willard; she had gotten a job as an assistant to his executive secretary.

Walters had a degree from Northwestern University in stage design and lighting although he wanted to be a director. After graduating, he had lived around Rush Street in Chicago where the closest he had come to getting a directing job was managing a comedy club. Because of his technical background, Charlene had convinced Willard to hire him to oversee the renovation of the King. Willard was unaware that they had had a sexual relationship in Chicago.

When Malcolm answered the door he was in his dressing gown and about to retire.

"Willard, is there something wrong? Can I help you?"

"Charlene's not home, Malcolm. Do you know where she is?"

"She's not here. She must still be at the theatre—though I can't imagine why."

"She was supposed to come home after she had changed and taken off her makeup. When she didn't arrive, I thought she might have had an accident on the road to our place, so I drove into town. Her car is outside the theater. The doors are locked, and there aren't any lights on—at least none that I could see."

"She might have gone home with another cast member, but I doubt it. She's not that close to the other actors. She could be downstairs in her dressing room. I saw a light under her door when I left."

"I don't have a key. Would you go over with me and let me in?" Willard asked.

"Of course, let me slip on some clothes."

As they spoke, a young man, about the same age as Walters, came out of the only bedroom in the small house; he was dressed only in silk shorts. "Malcolm, what's going on? Who's at the door?"

"It's Willard Carlisle. Charlene hasn't gotten home; he's worried. Willard, this is Tracey Eastin; we were all friends in Chicago. I'm sure Charlene has told you about him."

"Hello, Tracey. Yes, she's spoken of you." Willard's handshake was firm; it matched his stature and professional appearance.

"Tracey's my house guest. I asked him to take the train down from Chicago to help with the makeup and costumes."

"I'm glad you came," Willard replied. "Charlene is anxious to have people hear about the work she and Malcolm are doing here."

"Tracey, we're going over to the theatre to see if she's there."

"Do you want me to come?" Tracey asked.

"No, stay here; I'll be back in a few minutes. Willard, do you want me to drive?"

"Let's go separately," he replied. "I'll want my car to go home once we find her."

Willard and Eastin talked for a few minutes while Walters went back into the bedroom and put on a pair of jeans and a sweatshirt. It had turned cold outside, so he also picked up his jacket.

The men got in their separate cars and drove to the theatre. It was only about eight blocks. Belle Plaine, where the King Theater was located, had a population of a little more than twenty-six hundred, so everything was close to everything else.

They parked in front, near Charlene's car, and met at the door. Malcolm used his key. "Just stay put, Willard; I'll get some lights on." He walked to a panel against the far wall and threw a switch to illuminate the lobby.

They walked into the auditorium. Although it was dark, it was easy to find their way to the stage; several exit lights were on as well as a single light on a pole in the middle of the stage. It remained on when no one was in the theatre.

"Well, she's obviously not here," Malcolm said as they walked to the stage. "Let's go downstairs. I'll go first and get the lights." In deference to Willard, who was in his mid-sixties, he added, "Be careful, the stairs are a bit tricky." The wrought iron stairs leading down to the dressing rooms were black and circular.

With Willard following, Malcolm said, "Let's try the green room." When they didn't find her there, they moved on to the dressing rooms. Finally, they came to a door with a single star on it. It was Charlene's dressing room. There was light coming from under the door.

Malcolm knocked, "Charlene, are you here?" He tried the door. It wasn't locked. When he swung it open, Willard saw his wife lying on the floor with blood all over her head and upper torso. She was dead.

It was murder, and the Rounders would become deeply involved.

To find out when and how to obtain ***Murder In Three Acts*** go to the Rounders website:

www.Roundersmysteries.com

or

www.CLHutchins.com